PENGUIN METRO READS

BUFFERING LOVE

Issac John is a consumer marketing professional who turned to writing when a childhood dream surfaced far too often and he landed in New York to study screenwriting. On his return, he wore multiple hats of a columnist, teacher, Uber driver and consultant on the side while trying to hustle his way through a few manuscripts and screenplays. He counts Woody Allen, Jeffrey Archer, O'Henry, Hergé, Rajat Kapoor, Sai Paranjpe, David Mamet and Aaron Sorkin among his primary influences.

Prior to pursuing writing, Issac led the marketing team at PUMA India for four years. It was a job he loved dearly and his experiences there include sharing cookies with Roy Hodgson in the Directors' Box at the Emirates Stadium—the home of Arsenal Football Club, catching a beer with Usain Bolt and discussing the Ashes with Sachin Tendulkar. Notwithstanding these distractions, in 2015, *Pitch* magazine named Issac one of the Top 10 Young Marketers in India.

Issac currently heads marketing for HealthifyMe, one of India's leading health and fitness apps. He stays in Bengaluru with his wife and they both yearn to adopt a golden retriever and name him Captain Haddock.

BUFFERING

LOVE

STORIES FROM THE APP STORE

ISSAC JOHN

Penguin
metro reads

An imprint of Penguin Random House

PENGUIN METRO READS

USA | Canada | UK | Ireland | Australia
New Zealand | India | South Africa | China | Singapore

Penguin Metro Reads is part of the Penguin Random House group of companies
whose addresses can be found at global.penguinrandomhouse.com

Published by Penguin Random House India Pvt. Ltd
4th Floor, Capital Tower 1, MG Road,
Gurugram 122 002, Haryana, India

First published in Penguin Metro Reads by Penguin Random House India 2017

Illustrations by Parag Chitale

ISBN 9780143429487

Typeset in Adobe Garamond Pro by Manipal Digital Systems, Manipal
Printed at Repro India Limited

www.penguin.co.in

For my father, John K. Mathew, and his benign smile

*'Philip Morris just wanted your lungs.
The App Store wants your soul . . .'*

Bill Maher

Contents

Launched

Kabir loved stopping by Amy's place before going home every weekday. It was an escape he looked forward to indulging in after navigating the lows of being a start-up entrepreneur through the day.

They coordinated their rendezvous hours through a steady stream of messages on WhatsApp. Amy donned the hat of Principal at the hallowed venture capital firm of Lower Valley Capital that had recently set up operations in India. Meeting new entrepreneurs and assessing their business prospects was an everyday job for her. It was at the wedding of a common friend that she had first met Kabir—the young entrepreneur who was greying faster than most twenty-eight-year-olds.

Kabir, who was looking for his next round of funding, behaved like the perfect gentleman when he got Amy a dinner plate before taking one himself. As she extended her hand to take the plate, she thanked him. 'Let me wipe this for you with a napkin. The more extravagant a wedding appears, the worse the dinner plates,' he said.

Amy's perfect cheekbones sparkled with a pleasant smile at the unexpected gesture. 'And how many such wedding dinners have you been to?'

'Just one. Mine. Hated the plates but only saw them last minute. Wish they were cleaner. I am Kabir, by the way.' And that's how they ended up conversing late into the night. It helped that they were both without their respective partners.

Though Amy's firm was looking for new start-ups to invest in, she nipped Kabir's well-intentioned informal pitch over dinner with a curt response.

'We aren't looking to invest in media start-ups. The content boom was over two years ago. We are looking for cutting-edge innovations in education and health,' she proffered. After this, Kabir didn't say a word about his video content-based start-up called Play.

From her experience of dealing with Indian entrepreneurs so far, Amy thought Kabir would've ended the conversation there and moved on to his larger group of friends. It was the nature of her position that inevitably attracted attention from entrepreneurs. But once she turned down their propositions of funding needs, Amy observed that most Indian entrepreneurs didn't have the basic courtesy to even end the conversation on a friendly note.

In contrast to her experience in Silicon Valley, she had found the approach of Indian entrepreneurs to be completely transactional in nature. Kabir was a welcome change. He seemed interested in Amy's experiences of settling down in Mumbai. When she laughed at his silly observations of Mumbai's entrepreneurial playground, Kabir found himself drawn to her even more.

He gave her a list of bars to frequent, the best quaint coffee shops to have informal meetings in and little-known French bakeries spread around Khar and Bandra that served exquisite bread. Most importantly, he told her the whereabouts of a secret film club that he loved visiting on weekends. 'They have rare world cinema screenings on request. I'd be happy to take you there, if you want to go some time,' he suggested.

Amy loved only one thing more than her job, and that was discovering and rediscovering works of some of the world's greatest film-makers.

'I am going to take you up on that offer sooner than you know.' Her eyes sparkled.

When he walked Amy to her taxi that night, his hand grazed against her back that had bared itself rather invitingly with a little help from a black, sleeveless blouse. They both felt more than a flicker of raw inexplicable attraction, but there were too many common friends in sight who knew they were both married. They exchanged numbers with a promise to meet at the film club that weekend.

The next morning, Kabir received another refusal from a VC firm that, with its overtures of a multitude of data requests and presentations over the past three months, had seemed particularly keen to invest in Play. Crushed to bits, the only thought that sprang to his mind was to get away from work that evening. He told his twenty-member team that he was taking time off to focus on his next presentation over the weekend. What he wanted to do was to go to Qwench, his favourite quiet hotspot in a tiny lane in Bandra, and drink himself silly.

As he drove to Bandra from Juhu, he received a WhatsApp message from Amy. *'Hey, had a terrible week. Need to get away. When do you think we can go for the next screening at that film club?'*

The message took him by surprise. So much so that while taking a turn near Juhu beach, he nearly ran over what looked like a pedigreed chocolate-brown Labrador. The poor thing scurried away as Kabir applied the brakes in the nick of time. He parked his car towards the side and wrote back. 'It won't happen until Saturday afternoon. But if you like, I can come over with a Wong Kar-wai gem and a Californian red.'

'You are on. 7.30 p.m.,' she replied, appending her address to the message.

Her home, as luck would have it, was right next to Qwench. In ten minutes, with a Cabernet Sauvignon by his side, he was at her doorstep. She was wearing red overalls that reached her knees and sported a tinge of lipstick.

'Hey, that was quick!'

'I was just around the corner near Qwench, the bar, if you know it?'

'I don't. Do tell.'

'First, let's uncork this.'

The uncorking nearly undid their evening as the stubborn cork refused to part amicably from the bottle. When it finally fell apart in crumbs on the table, Kabir gently wiped off the remnants with one hand and let the crushed pieces fall on his other hand.

'Are you generally this particular, or is this a particular obsession?'

'A mess is not my idea of a good evening,' he replied. 'Let's sit outside in the balcony.'

They carried their glasses to the balcony and settled themselves amid the din of a city that wouldn't stop driving itself to its dreams. For the next few hours, Kabir and Amy bared their aspirations, fears and insecurities like two childhood friends meeting after a long time.

He spoke of his deep-seated ambition to make Play the definitive platform for short-form content in India. She spoke of her drive to expand business in India for Lower Valley Capital over the next five years with her newly assigned portfolios of health and education.

Amy saw in Kabir a spark that she had seen in many an entrepreneur in the Valley and in India. Except Kabir's had more of a childlike zeal, like a six-year-old with dreams to row his giant paper boat on a lake.

'In five years, long-form content as we know it in the form of two-hour films and hour-long television dramas will be wiped out. What will thrive is the genre of micro-stories, let's say sub-ten-minute content—films, music videos, fan-generated fiction, micro-blogs and what-not,' Kabir asserted.

'What's the maximum number of views you have had on any single video?'

'Anywhere between 3,00,000 and 4,00,000.'

'I agree with you. I think it's a great concept. What you probably also need right now is a tipping point, a video that helps you hit a million-plus views in a day. I have seen this in the US. The likes of BuzzFeed and Vice grew overnight because something went viral and then, of course, they got their formula right consistently.'

'What I need right now is for the desktop and mobile versions of Play to move to an app on iOS and Android Play Store. That's what I need the money for. If only someone in the VC community could see what I see.'

He stared into the blank night that lay before him and downed the last bit from his glass before asking her without a segue, 'Do you miss being alone here?'

'Why do you ask?'

'Because I have a wife here and yet this feels like such a lonely battle. This city subsumes you. I was wondering where that leaves you with your husband away in San Francisco.'

'Well, I do at times. But Rohan and I are very clear about what we want to do with our lives. He is running a cybersecurity firm out of the Valley right now, and I had this excellent opportunity to set up Lower Valley Capital here. We both needed to do this for our careers, and if a little distance was the price to pay, so be it.'

'I wouldn't call the distance between San Francisco and Mumbai "little", but I get it,' he said with a smile.

Their eyes met for the first time after a relentless rush of conversation. Since he had stepped into her house, their inquisitiveness for each other had got the better of time. Her dark eyes now bore a hint of a drunkenness that excited him.

Without notice, he leaned over and held her by the waist. She moved forward and sunk her lips into his. They didn't speak much for the next few hours.

Kabir left at 4 a.m. and bid her goodbye with a promise to meet again the next day.

For the next three months, whenever time permitted, they would go back to her balcony. Their meetings had no schedule. A no-fuss text of *Free tonight?* would decide the course of their rendezvous.

They always texted each other back instantly. There was an unerring rhythm to their exchanges. 'You know what I like about you the best?' she asked him one night.

'My gruff voice,' he played along.

'No, the fact that when we text each other, I know we are thinking of each other. I hate transactional messages. There's always more to our messages than what meets the eye. I don't look at you as a transaction.'

'But isn't every conversation a transaction? I mean not ours, but most of the day, that's what I deal in and yours isn't any different.'

'It isn't different, but it's worse for us. People keep coming to us for funds. Every conversation has a follow-up and when we lose interest, they don't strive to make any connection beyond the funds we bring to the table. It's like without our money, we are not people enough to be friends with. That's why I liked you that night.'

'What did I do?'

'You didn't go away with your friends even after I said that Lower Valley Capital won't have any funds for Play. You continued the conversation.'

'Anyone would've been a fool to go away from that conversation about films.'

'And yet you will be surprised how many people do.'

'That's because they are idiots.'

'Oh, I know they are,' she said and opened her mouth to plunge her tongue between his wide lips once again.

Just then, Amy's phone vibrated. It was a call from Rohan.

'I have to take this,' she said.

'When have I stopped you?' Kabir said without batting an eyelid as he caressed her neck.

Rohan had called to check if Amy's trip to San Francisco the following month was confirmed. Amy was having a difficult time focusing on the call, with Kabir's hands sliding inside her red top and tracing a curvy line all the way up to the hooks of her bra.

She could've used her hands to indicate Kabir to stop. Instead, she put on her earphones and clutched Kabir's wavy hair with her hands. She continued to kiss him while Rohan quickly gave her a set of dates that he would prefer for her to come to San Francisco. She threw her phone on the vacant cane chair the moment the call ended and started unbuttoning Kabir.

The number of wine bottles consumed every night increased gradually. Sometimes, they simply watched a Netflix film and went off to sleep. He would leave post-midnight or thereabouts. The fact that both of them had a working spouse went in their favour. Neither was emotionally invested enough yet to worry about larger consequences. This was a getaway, a vacation of an evening, each time. But in each other, they found a partner who could listen endlessly without prejudice and that's all that mattered.

One evening, an uncharacteristically chirpy Kabir called Amy. 'You won't believe what happened today.'

'Did you close a funding round?' She had never heard him so elated.

'I will tell you in person. Do you have time before your San Francisco flight?'

'We can meet at the airport.'

'Done. Starbucks, 11 p.m. Will see you there.'

Amy was already soothing herself with a cappuccino when Kabir walked in with a spring in his step. They hugged each other as they normally did. Even before they could sit, Kabir took his mobile phone out to show Amy a video.

'See the number of views?'

Amy looked at the number and, despite her strong background with numbers, took another look at the digits below a dog video posted on the Play website.

'Am I reading it right? Twelve *million* views!'

'That's correct. And it's not even been twenty-four hours. This is some girl in Mumbai and her chocolate-brown Labrador whom she clearly trained to use the flush. A fan-generated two-minute clip, and it's rocking our numbers today. Our organic registrations went through the roof!' Kabir couldn't stop gushing.

'That's quite something.'

'It's the tipping point. Your words. Remember? The one thing that tips the scales. I had been thinking about it and had recently added a section where fans could upload videos with their pets. The initial days saw no traction and suddenly the thing zoomed off. Last month we did 5,00,000-plus views on two cat videos. But this is a different beast altogether.'

Amy had never seen Kabir this enthused even about a Wong Kar-wai film. She was happy for him. She wanted to tell him that she was going to make a case for a funding for Play in any case, knowing so much about Kabir's business now.

She hadn't told him yet as it was a long shot. If anything, this new fan-generated section would only help make her case stronger with her boss, Marc Grazer. There was something in Kabir's happiness that made her happy. She almost wanted to lead his funding round, but she kept a calm demeanour. For the next hour, she continued to ask more questions about Play's specific financial models.

Before she left, she had a work request for him for the first time. 'Why don't you send me your latest pitch presentation along with your business plan for the next three years. I will bounce it off a few people in the Valley and see if anyone wants to talk business with you.'

This was an unexpected bounty for Kabir, the cherry on the cake on a day like this. They kissed each other goodbye like two lovers who weren't meant to be.

Over the next two weeks, Amy accompanied Marc, a flamboyant Valley entrepreneur, on a bunch of meetings he had lined up for her. She also spent time taking him through some of her initial groundwork on the health and education sectors in India. Marc was thoroughly impressed. Towards the end, she mentioned Play's recent tryst with content videos.

Marc, who had seen everything in the US, wasn't in the least bit impressed with yet another video content player. But he knew this was India and the price was likely to be cheap, very cheap.

'What do you think their closing ask is?'

'Play's pitch deck says 3 million USD, but I think they'd close for 2 million USD.'

That amount was peanuts for Marc. He only had one more question, 'And you like the entrepreneur's drive and vision?'

'I haven't seen anyone with so much zeal. Not even in the Valley. I can set up a meeting if this is of interest.'

'Are you nuts, Amy? I am not allocating any time for a two-million deal. But if you are convinced, go ahead and close it. India's bandwidth speeds will only increase and more and more people are going to consume video. I can take that bet on the market.'

Amy was thrilled for Kabir. What she had said about Kabir was true and he deserved the investment.

She wanted to tell Marc that she knew the entrepreneur only too well, and that she wouldn't want to lead the round for reasons of conflict of interest. But she thought it best to save it for later. She also had her hands full with a few education and health tech start-ups and would've anyway needed to transfer Play's deal to a colleague.

Amy was also able to spend a good amount of time with Rohan. Knowing that she was going to be in town, he had taken time off work and prepared breakfast every day for her. Most days, as she munched the organic muesli and wolfed down the eggs, her thoughts continued to veer towards Kabir.

They kept in touch through short calls and messages that only indicated that Kabir was developing feelings for Amy. 'Can't wait to get back to our balcony,' he would often say.

'Our' balcony—the thought did not seem alien to Amy any more. She wanted to get back to him at the earliest and give him news of Lower Valley Capital's interest in Play.

That's when destiny took an unexpected turn.

One of Marc's most high-profile start-up investments called Blink—a photo-sharing app—went bankrupt. Since he required help on all fronts to shore up last-minute liquidation efforts, he asked Amy to stay back longer.

'It will take another four weeks, at best. Since everything that you are handling is still in the early stages, you can help me deal with this mess first. In the meantime, let the APAC office handle your India decisions for the time being.'

On the one hand, Amy was upset that it would be another month before she could meet Kabir, but on the other, she was happy that the Asia-Pacific office could deal directly with Kabir and she wouldn't have to bring up the issue of the conflict of interest of her knowing Kabir only too well. She wanted the deal to be as clean as possible.

That evening, she finally broke the news to him that she had to stay back for another month. 'I can't wait to get back either, but it's just . . . Marc really needs me here and I couldn't say no.'

Kabir was crestfallen. He was looking forward to seeing her. As his funds dried up, Amy was the only sliver of brightness in his life. And that's when that sole sliver of light sprung up to brighten his day. 'And listen, I spoke to Marc about Play. He is interested and has directed the APAC office to get in touch with you. You will have a pitch next week. Get your numbers ready and make them solid. If they like you, they could go all in with a 2-million USD round.'

Kabir couldn't believe the sound of it. 'But I thought you said Marc's company won't do content start-ups?'

'He wouldn't have. If not for me. But you can thank me for it later. On *our* balcony.'

After the call, Kabir sat down to come to terms with all that he suddenly had on his plate. He had a lot to accomplish for the meeting next week. After three rounds of video conferences, the APAC team flew Kabir down to Hong Kong in a month's time for a final Investment Committee meeting. The verdict was unanimous: Play had a solid future and Lower Valley Capital was going to invest 2 million USD.

That night Kabir and Amy talked for hours on a WhatsApp call. She couldn't have enough of his voice and he couldn't stop either.

Meanwhile, Amy's US visit was extended by another month and Kabir went full steam ahead with the plans of his app launch on both the Play Store and App Store.

'I will be there in July,' she declared to Kabir. 'Let's go someplace you and I can get some time together.'

For the first time, Kabir hesitated to reciprocate. 'I am not sure, Amy. It might be peak launch time for the app.'

Amy understood and didn't press further. Both of them were consumed with work over the next month. Finally, when she took off from San Francisco, she was delighted as she put her headphones on. Mumbai was beginning to seem like home now.

When she landed, Kabir wasn't there to pick her up as he had promised.

'There's been a major tech snag. I need to be here. But I will see you tomorrow, won't I?'

Amy didn't have it in her to tell him to come right away. She said yes softly. Her jetlag was troubling. She spent the night watching a Wong Kar-wai film.

The app launch was a big deal for Kabir. He had barely managed a wink of sleep. Towards the end of the day, he texted her. *Tomorrow, you and I, out on the town.'*

She replied, *'When?'*

'I will meet you at 7 p.m. for a quick drink. We launch at 9 p.m. I will be in office to cut a cake and then leave to pick you up.'

'Sounds like a plan. Finally. ☺ *'*

Kabir could almost hear her smile. The next day, Amy was too tired to go to office. She worked from home and beamed as the clock struck seven. Right on cue, the doorbell rang.

It was the newspaper vendor, wanting to clear his bill of the past two months.

'So sorry, got delayed. I will text you at 10 p.m. and we'll fix a place,' read a text from Kabir when she got back to her mobile phone.

This was the first time an exchange with Kabir had sounded like a transaction.

Play took off that night with one of the best launches in the history of apps in India. She spent the evening on *their* balcony, waiting for his text at 10 p.m. After waiting restlessly for over an hour, finally at 11.20 p.m., she messaged to ask if he wanted to come over.

He never replied.

Video Star

If you met me for the first time, you would think I couldn't talk very well. Every woof of mine would seem identical to you. But that's because you are not Navya. If you spoke to her, she would tell you that my vocabulary is damn good.

How I met Navya is a long story, but I will crunch it down. Let me put it this way, she was not the first of my conquests.

That came out wrong, didn't it? Let's rewind. Woof!

I was born in a pack of four or five. Or maybe six. I could never count right. I struggled with my siblings to get my share of mom's milk and it always seemed more crowded than four then. Anyway, I digress. But as a chocolate-brown Labrador, you must know, digression is what I live for. Where was I? Ah . . .

It was the summer of 2010 and I was barely three. My dog collar proclaimed my name—Julius. I even had a ten-digit mobile number attributed to me. Not that I ever needed it. A phone is the last thing I had any use for. Meanwhile, something bad was brewing in the West according to the papers. 'Downturn', 'housing collapse' and 'mortgages' were words I often heard my owners, Rashi and Akshay, bandy about in our house at the NCPA Apartments in Nariman Point.

'What are the chances that the Lester Brothers would go bust?' I heard Rashi ask Akshay one night as they lay side by side in bed.

'I think we are going down a 100 per cent,' Akshay said, before turning over to the other side.

'How will we afford this apartment?' she pressed.

'We'll see, I don't know,' Akshay's reply barely registered.

The next morning, I was back on the promenade with Akshay for my morning walk, bottom-sniffing every breed that came my way. This is why I loved Nariman Point; for the breeze and for Akshay by my side while I cavorted aimlessly.

And then, three months later, God knows why, we moved houses. Our new house was an unlovable shack in a new place called Andheri. I had never been there before and I suppose I aged a decade in human years during that never-ending drive. Let me tell you, it is not a safe place to walk for us dogs. Vegetable vendors, locksmiths and cobblers splayed themselves across the footpath and terribly loud trains ran overhead without notice. If there was a civilization whose finest achievement was cacophony, Andheri was it.

But it wasn't just Andheri that gave me the creeps. I once saw Rashi sob on the cushions on the couch all alone. When I went to her, she hugged me tight. It made me queasy.

One night after Akshay came back, they spoke to each other in high-pitched voices. It seared my eardrums and the next thing I knew, Akshay kissed me and walked out alone in the middle of the night. I stood at the door all night, waiting for him to come back, but he didn't.

My walks became shorter every day with Rashi. She would run out of breath in ten minutes. I didn't like it any more. If you are a dog (and I most certainly hope you are), you know what I mean. We like long walks, long runs and long fetch missions. Don't hang a ball in a bathroom over our head and ask us to fetch it from the bedroom—it's insulting.

I was unhappy and I could see Rashi was unhappy too. But what I liked about her was that she still made the effort. One fine morning, she took me in her car to a large water place. You might have seen swimming pools in your lifetime but you don't know about this one. It was like this massive swimming pool of waves that kept thudding into the sands ashore. This was *nuts*!

The huge waves kept slamming me in my face and I loved it. Rashi took me off the leash. To be honest with you, there can't be a bigger swimming pool than this one. We had one in our apartment complex back at Nariman Point, but that was like a drop in the ocean compared to this.

What a happy day it was! I licked the hell out of Rashi's ears that day, but I could still see her crying. It was the first time my slobbery kisses didn't dry her tears. Later that evening, we sat down on the sand and I felt the breeze on my nostrils. It carried with it that salty waft of popcorn that put me to sleep.

When I opened my eyes, I couldn't find Rashi. I ran up and down the long stretches of sand. Was I dreaming? No, of course not. Someone had taken her away from me. I tried to follow the trail of her smell to the car. But our compact four-wheeler wasn't around. It was mysterious. Someone had taken Rashi away from me and flicked the car. Jeez, Rashi. I hope she got home all right.

Stupid me, how could I sleep off? And what about my supreme power of smell? Couldn't I trace her back? I still had my collar on me. Oh gosh, what did I do!

I roamed around wherever the sands of this large new swimming pool took me. I found some friends occasionally. Some were rather aggressive and my friendly bottom-sniffs towards these dogs were met with fierce growling. Once, a lumbering Rottweiler even leapt to try and bite me.

This wasn't pleasant any more. The popcorn now started smelling stale every day and if I ever ventured towards the road, I found it awfully difficult to get to the other side. Once, a car almost ran over me. I preferred the sands compared to the loud honks on the road and decided to make it my home. And then, one day, I saw this girl come running towards me.

I have had human kids run towards me before and I always let them hug me, pat me or just stroke my forehead but this one did something very few kids do. She went for my belly. It was almost embarrassing with so many people looking at me. I mean, not that I didn't like it. I *lurvved* it. I am not one for much PDA but this girl, boy oh boy, she was totally risqué in wooing me. I closed my eyes and lifted my paws and that's when I heard a name—Navya—her parents called out to her.

She was taking a stroll on the beach with her mom, Sarika, and dad, Roshan.

Well, then what, you ask? I went for the jugular. I sprang upon her parents. And they patted me and stroked my forehead and chin. Everything but the belly. I guess they were a little conservative that way.

And then her dad went away for some time while Navya and her mom hung out with me. It was time for me to meet my other friends near the large swimming pool for snacks but

I didn't mind being with the family here. And then her father returned. *With.a.leash*.

'Get outta here! That's the same leash Rashi had! Will you take me to Rashi?'

I had a ton of questions buzzing through my head. The leash smelt different though. Like new. Navya knelt down and lovingly put it around my neck. Wait a minute. Was Nayva going to take me for a walk? Like the good old days with Akshay? I had no clue, but I leapt ahead with the thought and she sprinted instinctively with me on the sand. The wind hit us in our faces. We looked at each other. I knew I was in love with her.

The next thing I know I was in a new car and had landed in a new home with a nice corner underneath the stairs. Then came a new bedsheet, a new water bowl and a new food bowl along with a new name: Max!

She must've been about ten or eleven, maybe. Or twelve. I don't know. Counting wasn't ever my forte. I had a little girl taking care of me now and it had never happened to me before. Both Akshay and Rashi were grown-ups, but Navya was different. She had so much time for me! We were now in Juhu, by the way. I liked this hip neighbourhood way better than Andheri.

How I loved my Sundays. It was time spent in the sun and rolling on the sand on that beach Navya and her parents had found me on.

A few months later, they sent me for training. It was so much fun. It was with this sweet blonde lady who took us to a park near the house. I even had some classmates for company—terriers, dachshunds, Great Danes—oh Lord,

I can't even recall the others. Now, that was my kind of party and don't even get me started on the treats.

Every day was a riot. First, we trained in the park and then at home. But, you see, I was a little ahead of the class. A canine prodigy in the heart of Juhu, you could say.

The terrier and I would often compare notes at the end of each class about how many treats each pooch got. I was way ahead of the others. I guess the trainer told mom and dad about me, and soon this sweet trainer started coming home. I missed my friends from the park, but advanced education can get lonely at the top. You can't have a world-class thesis without a solitary existence. But you also can't have a world-class protégé without a master like Navya.

As smart as the trainer was, I was only interested in wooing Navya. When her friends came home, she would strut me around and make me go through all the commands. 'Sit', 'Leave', 'Stay', 'Newspaper', 'TV Remote' and what not. I knew them all by heart. Every time I followed the rhythm of her voice she would come running to me to give me a chin rub. Apparently, during these sessions I was 'Good boy Max'.

'Good Boy' is like knighthood for us dogs. We don't know what it does, but we want it. I was Navya's Good Boy. At night, she hugged me close when she slept. I often woke up in the middle of the night only to see if she was sleeping soundly. She never told me explicitly but I saw her doing the same for me too. I pretended I was asleep. I had to try hard to not wag my tail during those moments.

While at class, I was taught a few more advanced tricks. Like standing on my hind legs up to a count of ten. And that trainer, oh God, what delightful hands she possessed. Her belly rubs were legendary! Like a bae gone rogue. The most difficult thing I learnt from her was when she taught me how to sit like humans and do the pee-pee. It was Mission Impossible but that insane belly rub got me going.

I had difficulty perching myself in the initial days, but it was a piece of cake afterwards. OMG! The treats you would get if you just did that once. And then if you also stood up and pressed a button that would bring a gush of water, it was like getting laid and eating fried chicken at the same time.

My going to the bathroom impressed Navya and mom and dad because at every party they would make me do it. All the humans would line up to watch. Once I pressed the button that brought the water, I could see everyone laugh and give me those coochy-coos and good-boy invocations all over again.

Truth be told, I wasn't too fond of that excess attention. But a little exhibitionism for Navya and mom and dad for the love they showered on me was nothing.

It was great for a few years. And then, one day, I felt a pain in my leg, the left hind leg to be specific. Then magically, the pain spread to my other legs as well. I didn't like those long walks any more. I preferred shorter ones. I could still do my tricks in the bathroom but not the toilet trick any more. Mom and dad understood that.

Navya was growing up like a wild mushroom. She was much taller than me now. Imagine there used to be a time when we both stood at the same height. It was her fifteenth birthday when a lot of her friends came home. After everyone left, mom and dad entered our room (well, Navya's room technically) and gifted her a rectangular device in a white box that had the image of a half-eaten apple on it. I had seen Akshay and Rashi use that device very often.

You might know what I am talking about. These humans, they bring this thing to the ear and then talk to it. Honestly, I don't know what the fuss is about. We dogs do just fine without it.

But Navya was happy and fiddled with it all day. She started spending less time with me now.

Earlier, she would come from school and we would raid the house for goodies, but she began to skip that routine. She would keep staring at this device. She traded those chin rubs for me with swipes and clicks on that thing. At times, I would lay by her feet and lick her to remind her that I was around, but boy was she addicted to this! She would also be so tired peering into this thing before sleeping that she stopped waking up to check on me like she used to. Not that it made any difference to me. I was still waking up to see if she was sleeping tight.

But Navya also turned a little cuckoo. Without notice, she would come near me and bring that device right to my face. I would eagerly bring myself closer to her, and suddenly all I would hear was the sharp sound of a click. The click made me crazy. She would call my name and, bang, the thing would go click. It was like the sound of a shutter opening and closing in quick succession.

Then she would show me how I looked on that device. I had seen myself in mirrors before but my tail was always wagging; I could see it. But on this device, my tail stood still. Phew, wasn't that sick!

Most of my moments were captured on that device, like time that had gone by but frozen and shoved in your face. How's that for magic? Cool, right? Well, it was all Navya, she was a magical girl.

There was also this thing they kept calling a video. Every conversation about her friends on that device was about this video, that video, Gangnam video, cat video. Such craze, I tell ya, with everyone peering into similar devices and looking at videos.

One day, while Navya was busy with her homework, she called out my name repeatedly. She wanted me to sit on the toilet. I knew that sign. Did she really want me to sit on the toilet seat again? I wanted to tell her that it was getting painful but it was Navya, so I tried.

I couldn't get going the first couple of times, but there I was on my fourth attempt. I tucked my little butt against the back of the toilet and placed my legs on the seat and relieved myself. I was shivering with anxiety. A little push and my knees would've given way. But, hey, I came through.

Navya was chuffed to bits, I could tell. Though she didn't exactly see me doing it, she had that device with her and was looking at me through it. Was it a video she was taking? I hope she doesn't show the bad parts of me trying to get on top of that toilet seat to her friend. Especially to that hot one called Rachel who smells like chocolate all day long. I mean I had greyed but I had my eye on her for a belly rub.

Anyway, I forgot all about it. Next thing I know, she was showing that video to all her friends who came home later that evening. How do I know? Well, that water gushing sound. It always played towards the end. Remember, I always pressed that button? They would all get together and look at that device, and they would also look it up on the computer. I think they had saved it on the computer or something.

Every evening, she would sit on the computer and look at that video of mine. Like I told you, I am not good at maths, but that's when I try and count for myself. When a number is written in front of me, I can read it like Einstein. I looked at the number that appeared below my video. First it was 900 something, the next day it was 33,000 something, and then a week later it was 5,00,000 something. That stupid video of me taking a leak had got so many views.

One fine day, her photo appeared in the newspaper. *'Juhu girl's pet video rakes up 12 million views in 2 days.'* Her shrieks of delight that filled the house were like nothing I had ever heard before. I was happy for her. But those idiots had put my picture up with my willy too! I didn't have a problem with it. If grown men and women enjoy peeking at my willy, who am I to stop them? I sure as hell don't want to look at any man's (or woman's) nether regions.

But you know what I had a problem with? Navya wouldn't even look at me any more without holding up this device. Even if she took me out for a walk, she would be staring at it. Sometimes it was a video and sometimes it was that clicking sound. Same thing every day. She stopped looking at me with her wistful eyes like she used to when she was young. It had been days since she had patted me or even touched me. I hated it. I wanted that device out of my life.

One day while she was on her computer, again looking at that video of mine, I sneaked behind her, took that device in my mouth and ran around the house. She came running after me.

'There we go. Now we are playing, Navya. Just like the old days,' I wagged my tail furiously to get her into the mood. She liked it too.

She chased me around the dining table as I ran in circles. I was old, but I still had some steam left in the tank. Feeling a little giddy, I charged towards the bathroom.

I sensed her voice becoming a little hoarse as I came near the toilet. She reached out for the phone, but I wanted to win this round. I swung my head away and dunked that damned device in the toilet. And you know about my training right, by sheer instinct I stood up to press the button through which water gushed out.

Navya let out a terrible, blood-curdling squall. She screamed my name as I shrunk into a corner. Was she angry?

'Oh, come on. You know how many years we spent together before that thing came in between. You don't even look at me any more. You just look at me through it,' I reasoned with her, wagging in submission. I even took my tail right between my legs to diffuse the crisis.

She went for my head and, in one unexpected sweep of her hand, thrust me neck-deep into the water in the toilet. I couldn't breathe. I couldn't believe what was happening.

'Navya, please, this is hurting. Don't do this, please,' I yelped.

I let out an obnoxious gurgle. A deluge of water went right up to my lungs. I could sense they were bursting inside. I was dying. This is it. But she kept yelling.

'I was better off on that beach all by myself. I wish I had never met this girl,' was the last thought that buzzed in my head before she yanked me out of that water and flung me on the chequered tiles.

My heavy head thudded on the cold floor. She walked away in a huff while I lay gasping for breath.

A part of me was devilishly happy that she had touched me after so many days.

Email à Trois

Professor Albert Costanza was the quintessential aloof professor at the National School of Drama, whose mind was interested in a conversation with common folk only if the other person did one of the following two things:

1. They gave him a cinematic reference or a dialogue that he didn't know.
2. They made a joke about the name Albert that did not invoke the old Hindi film *Albert Pinto Ko Gussa Kyun Aata Hai*.

Truth be told, he was beginning to get tired of the Albert Einstein jokes too. So, when the new professor of French cinema, Navya Ojha, affectionately referred to Prof. Albert as Albert Camus, his joy knew no bounds.

That week had also been particularly tough on the Costanza family because his wife, a reasonable woman in her forties, had been exceptionally nagging that week. During a mid-week fight, the professor had threatened to leave her but knowing that he had no possessions to fall back on, except his wife's car and house, he timidly decided to stay put.

Besides, the thought of being companionless for the rest of his life, thanks to his receding hairline and burgeoning waistline, he surmised it was best to stick with the wife.

When you are in your fifties, developing a physical attraction to anything living or dead is just too much hard work and effort. Yet, Ms Ojha's colourful saris and her young, supple neckline were working their wonders on Prof. Costanza's mind. That Ms Ojha was more than a decade younger only exaggerated his pining.

Hence, on the first Friday of June 2017, Prof. Costanza walked up to Ms Ojha to ask her out for an evening of drinks at the nearby Irish Bar, Bennigans.

Many an e-mail guru will speak to you folks about the potential miscommunication possible when people rely solely on e-mails to prove a point in heavy-handed corporate discussions. The following is an account of the aftermath of that cheerful and terrific evening as documented on e-mail by Prof. Costanza, one of the brightest academic minds on Indian cinema.

Readers may bear in mind that the personal email address handed to Prof. Costanza on a paper napkin by Ms Ojha at the end of the evening was navya0@gmail.com. This the professor specifically requested because he wanted to write an ode to Navya. After exchanging numerous giggles and a jolly good evening of drunken stupor, by the time Prof. Costanza sat on his writing chair, he read the email address as navyao@gmail.com, thus, beginning an adventure of a lifetime.

From: Albert Costanza <albert.costanza@gmail.com>

To: Navya <navyao@gmail.com>

Date: Sunday, 4 June 2016

Subject: Can't . . .

Mailed by: nsd.edu

Navya,

I waited for a couple of days before putting this down. I wanted to be far away from the halo I felt emanating from you that Friday evening. I can't say I have gotten too far though. In cosmic terms, it's only a weekend that's passed us by. For me, it has been an eternity.

And there's this bittersweet pain now because I don't know if I will ever meet you again as a friend or as a lover.

Your smile that could disarm a tyrant has been haunting me since Friday. And even then, it wasn't your smile but something brattishly silly about you that caught my fancy.

Since childhood, whenever I told people that my name was Albert, an inevitable (witless) response from people from this part of the world was this single question: 'Pinto, huh?' It is such a ridiculous trying-so-hard-to-be-funny comment that in my mind I have reserved the scummiest of looks for such people. Of late, I have even begun to use this as a filter to judge humanity in general.

Why not spring up Albert Schweitzer on me? Or that fella Finney, he is still around, isn't he? Even Einstein, I had come to accept. Alas! Everyone was so utterly predictable, every single one of them.

Anyone exclaiming 'Pinto!' as a smart comeback in an introduction was tolling the very death knell of our relationship. I wasn't ever going to be friends with someone like that. It's not just been a rule of thumb. It has been the iron-clad rule of all my ten fingers combined.

That's why, when I met you that day in the staff room and your comeback to my name was 'Camus?', I knew you were different. I mean it in more ways than one.

When I asked you out this Friday, you smiled and told me that you would give it a good think. Sitting in my office for the next half an hour was agonizing. As a man of science and arts, I sat there praying that you don't get any other dates that evening. That something pulls you back towards me and we could step out. But who was I kidding. It was Friday and nobody is busier in New Delhi on a Friday evening than an attractive French cinema educationist.

I killed my expectations and got down to work on that stupid exam paper I had to set.

When my phone rang, I had to pinch myself to confirm that I wasn't dreaming. It was you! I ran down the stairs and hopped across the lawn. I had never felt like that about any lady before.

I noticed something different about you. You had done up your hair, added a shade of lipstick and were wearing a brown jacket. Did you just go home to get ready for the evening? I hoped my Nehru jacket would complement your leather.

The last time this happened was when I had kissed my first crush in school. A kiss today was the last thing on my mind. I just wanted to spend some time with you. I wanted to hold on to each second from there on. It was 8.30 p.m. then, wasn't it?

From there on, we cabbed it, we had dinner, we walked down the markets of Greater Kailash-1 and 2, and we drank and we danced. We went our separate ways at 2 a.m.

Between those hours, you told me about your child, your marriage, your filthy-rich shipping magnate date, your divorce, your business, your education, London, your pole-dancing party, your Asian friends and your musical proclivities. I listened like they were the last few hours before the Apocalypse would engulf me. In between, you held my hand and pulled me through the crowd at Pianos. If I had a heart any feebler, I would've died right then. I had a plunging fear that I had to behave absolutely normal with you. I didn't want to mess anything up that day. I wanted you to feel for me, just like I did.

It was just us that evening. Just as I had hoped and prayed. Fittingly, we parted at a delicatessen, like Harry and Sally in the movie. Like I told you, my evening was a lot better than I could've bargained for.

I don't know about you. Chances are this was a very usual evening for you. You have seen more shades of life than I have. You have suffered more than I have. To think that someone like you could go through so much pain because of people close to you was a very troubling thought for me.

Yesterday evening, I kept thinking of you as I walked around Greater Kailash. This time I decided to go to a Comedy Club to get you out of my head. For the record, it was the dumbest thing I have embarked upon. It has been three days now and I can't get you off my mind.

I know you need stability. You are itching for that family. We are two poles apart. And the sides we inherit aren't even on the same field. And yet, I would feel stupid if I didn't let you know how much you meant to me that evening.

I am not on the best of talking terms with my wife, but if you find it within yourself to live a life with me, say the word, and I will come running to you. But I need that first sign from you to take things ahead.

This infinitesimal existence of ours could do with people loving more people. That's all I know, and I will change everything around me, in me, to be with you.

I know I will have no say in whether we will ever be in touch again. For once, I wish I had the world-changing power of Einstein's mind and could convince you to remain in touch with me. But

I know this: To meet you again, I would even be fine being a Pinto. Or whatever you would like to call me for the evening.

> *Yours,*
> *Albert*

But navyao@gmail.com belonged to Navya Oberoi, a fifteen-year-old spoilt brat from Mumbai. She had just got over 12 million views on a video she took of her dog flushing the toilet. She was unfettered in spirit and remorseless with the power of this new-found fame on Instagram.

Without a moment's hesitation in pulling off a prank, she deviously replied:

From: Navya Oberoi <navyao@gmail.com>
To: Albert Costanza <albert.costanza@gmail.com>

Date: Sunday, 4 June 2016

Subject: Re: Can't…

Mailed by: gmail.com

Albert,

I want to do this with you. Let's marry each other. I know I am convinced.
    Show me that you are too.

Best and love,
Navya

From there on, Navya Oberoi went about her life taking more videos of her dog on Instagram.

That night, Prof. Costanza broached the topic of separation with his wife. He cited her high-handed monopoly over his time as the single largest contributing factor to the decision. His wife, who was equally irritated with the professor's long hours away from home, didn't bat an eyelid and threatened him with a raging alimony demand that would make him bankrupt in no time. The professor couldn't care less and stomped out of the house in the middle of the night with his sole possession, a 1989 Remington typewriter, in tow. It was the image of a man blinded by love and passion, a modern-day Trojan prince like Paris who would pay any price for his Helen.

Meanwhile, Prof. Navya Ojha waited all of that weekend for the ode that Prof. Costanza said he was going to send her way. Since it never came, she thought it only good manners to send a thank-you note to him.

From: Navya Ojha <navya0@gmail.com>
To: Albert Costanza <albert.costanza@gmail.com>

Date: Sunday, 4 June 2016

Subject: Thank you

Thank you, Prof. Albert, for such a lovely evening. In this alien city, I was almost starving for that brotherly affection that you showered on me.

This city aches me with its near-perverted touches towards its women, but the gentlemanly way in which you dealt with

me reminded me so much of my own brother, Sarang, who I
had mentioned had passed away in aerial combat during the
Kargil War. Even your loving face is but a pleasing souvenir of
his countenance.

It was divine providence that brought my beloved Sarang
back into my life in your form, Prof. Albert Costanza. Or would
you prefer Prof. Pinto? (Teehee . . . teehee)

Your (new) beloved sister,
Navya

Winner Takes All

After the celebrations of his seventieth birthday at Gratitude Old Age Home, Shankar was a little subdued. Normally the life of a party, Shankar cut the cake with a mild tremor in his hands, the fallout of a much-vaunted bout against Parkinson's disease that just wouldn't leave his side.

His best friend, Damodar, however, had a glint in his eyes. With a few furtive calls to Shankar's sixteen-year-old granddaughter, Navya, who stayed in Mumbai, he had managed to get her to come to Bangalore this evening as a surprise.

It was all settled. Navya was used to travelling alone since she had turned fifteen, thanks to her father trusting her companion—a mobile phone.

'As long as we are in touch with her, there is no harm in her visiting her grandfather every year for the vacations,' Roshan reasoned with his wife, Sarika.

Gratitude was unlike any other old-age home. The rooms were more than adequate, equipped with a fridge, a couch, a DVD Player with TV and a mammoth bed. It wasn't Roshan's idea to put up Shankar in an old-age home, but after his wife died, Shankar decided not to leave Bengaluru. When Roshan moved to Mumbai because of a new job, he insisted that Shankar move with him, but Shankar was way too stubborn.

'This is where my friends are. What more do I need than to play a round of bridge and carom with Damodar every evening followed by a late-night film. Mumbai is not for me. Not at this age for sure.'

Roshan relented.

With time, Shankar had got over his wife's death. If anything, he mildly relished the attention from the neighbourhood ladies post her death. The only missing piece in Shankar's life was not getting to spend time with Navya.

He considered Mumbai, ever so briefly, only for Navya's sake. But again, the girl wouldn't have time for him in a busy city. More so, when in a single week, apart from her academics she had football and music classes to attend. Thus, Shankar throttled his desire to move cities and instead chose the hearth at Gratitude.

Today, on his seventieth birthday, Shankar felt like killing himself. Before coming out of the room to cut the cake, he stared at the ceiling fan and wondered how much time it would take to tie a bedsheet like they did in films. His reverie was interrupted by a knock on the door.

'Next round of bridge begins. Get out,' hollered Damodar.

'I want to sleep,' a disinclined Shankar muttered.

But Damodar was unyielding. He kept banging on the door.

Shankar stood up in a huff to call off on his friend. As he unbolted the craggy door, he heard an unusual voice.

Right outside stood Navya with a heavy backpack on her shoulders. She lunged at Shankar with both her arms, almost throwing the old man off his feet.

'Appppaaaa! Happy birthday!'

'That's why you should listen to your friend. No matter whatever the time of the day,' a boastful Damodar pronounced.

Shankar could barely acknowledge this little act of kindness from his friend because in Navya's presence there was a peace that he hadn't experienced in a while.

'Thank you, Damodar. This could be too good for my heart,' he spoke with a hint of moisture in his eyes.

Damodar, too, almost welled up. Next month, he was to travel to Mumbai to meet his grandson on his eighteenth birthday. His estranged daughter wouldn't send him to Bengaluru but agreed to Damodar visiting. 'I'll leave you two now. See you guys later,' he said before leaving.

'Appa, look what I got for you,' Navya handed him a box that was evidently wrapped in love as much as that glossy silver paper.

'Did Roshan send you alone?'

'Later, Appa, open this and see no . . .' she urged him.

Shankar saw a gleaming iPad in front of him. 'What will I do with this?'

'I asked Papa what to get you for your seventieth, and he mentioned that you used to be an avid quizzer in your college days.'

'Not just college, darling,' Shankar said in a bid to correct her.

'So I got to know. Anyway, what I have put in this iPad for you is this app called Quiz-Up, where you can play quizzes all day long.'

'Quizzing is no fun without a partner,' Shankar mused. 'Not that I don't like it.'

'But that's the cool thing about Quiz-Up, Appa. You can play it with anybody,' an excited Navya proceeded to open the app. 'See, here you can select the topics, and once you have done that, each topic has seven questions. You attempt to answer each question in the least possible time. The faster you answer, the more points you get. See, this is the leader board for Bengaluru. As you play against other people and get points, you keep climbing up the ranks here.'

Shankar peered into the screen and saw a certain 'Fiery Granny' ranked as #1 in Bengaluru under the category of Movies. That irritated him a bit already. Surely, getting to the top of the Bengaluru leader board was worth living for, he pondered.

For the next couple of hours, Navya spoke about her school and her football classes and Shankar couldn't take his attention away from her. Once she retreated for a nap, he started fiddling around with the iPad in general and the Quiz-Up app in particular. Nayva had already set up a user name for Shankar: Dr Cool.

While the app was full of topics that ranged from specific episodes in famous TV series to Wars to Sports, Shankar went for a personal favourite: 'Movies: General'. The DVD player in his room had been put to good use in the recent months.

His first opponent was a Luke Wilson, whom he dismissed with arrogance with a dominating score. The next was a lady called Demon555 who came his way. No problem dispatching her either.

His next opponent was Fiery Granny, the top-ranked quizzer in Bengaluru as per the app.

Shankar was able to beat her with a 200 to 180 score. This was the closest anyone had got to Shankar's score in the last ten minutes. He pushed for one more game.

Shankar was on the money for the first three questions. But so was Fiery Granny. The score was tied at 60 each.

And then Fiery Granny zoomed ahead on the next two questions to be at 100 while Shankar, in spite of being right, lagged behind with 84. The next question was one that Shankar would never forget since he had reviewed it for *The Hindu*.

Who essayed the role of Chief Judge Dan Haywood in the war classic *Judgement at Nuremberg*?

A)   Spencer Tracy
B)   Gregory Peck
C)   Montgomery Clift
D)   Burt Lancaster

The app rewarded users with extra points if one answered quickly. This is where Shankar could race ahead if he clicked on Spencer Tracy in time. He smirked at the thought of bridging that gap of sixteen points with a click.

Right then, thanks to Shankar's poor Internet connection, the app hung. It just wouldn't move. He involuntarily let out a sheepish shriek, careful enough to not wake up Navya.

He couldn't load the next two questions either. While Shankar fiddled around to check what was wrong, the next screen that came up announced that Fiery Granny had won the round. Shankar asked for a rematch with the same opponent but got a notification that Fiery Granny had left the game.

Shankar tossed aside the iPad and spent the rest of the evening playing carom with Navya and taking a long walk around the lush colony of Sadashivnagar with her.

'Why don't you come to Mumbai and stay with us, Appa? Papa tells me you don't want to,' Navya mentioned in passing while feasting on her masala dosa later that evening.

'I can't leave the city. I would much rather leave this world,' Shankar mused with a smile.

'Why would you ever say that?'

'I am kidding. But really, this is where I grew up. And this city gave me my friends and my wife. I almost feel like I would be betraying them if I left.'

'What about me? Don't you think we can have a good time together if you stay with me? Don't you miss me?'

'I do. Every single day. You have no clue what your visit meant to me this time. I was really missing you, but you have your life there, your classes, your dancing and football and friends. You are at an age where you should be spending more time with them, not me.'

The next morning Navya left for Mumbai and Shankar once again felt that biting loneliness in his gut as he came back to his room. Yes, Damodar and the rest of the residents here were all fond of him, and he was nothing less than a ladies' man, but he had started viewing every social interaction as a pain.

He wanted to evade negative thoughts so he let his hand wander over to the slick iPad that lay beside him. He swiped over the first couple of screens and his eyes rested on Quiz-Up. There was a little number that hung over the icon. Having never received a notification before, Shankar wondered if it might be an extra point from the games he played yesterday.

As he opened the app, it turned out to be a message from Fiery Granny. And it read: *'Chicken!'*

Shankar fumed. He understood this as a reference to his battle of wits with her yesterday when he couldn't finish the game because of the Internet connection. But what cheek the woman had to call him 'chicken'. It particularly hurt Shankar when he saw that Fiery Granny's profile picture was that of an eagle.

He pressed the reply button and sent a rather confrontational message: '*11.30 a.m. Best of 5. Let's decide this once and for all.*'

He immediately received two messages from Fiery Granny. One said: '*Done.*'

The other said, '*Catch you soon, chicken.*'

Shankar hated this reference but knowing that the best comebacks are those saddled with action, he thought of dealing with this insult after the game. If he defeated her, he would have a much larger share of the bragging rights.

Never in the last one year that he had been at Gratitude did Shankar seethe this intensely. He was a man on a mission to annihilate Fiery Granny. Little did Fiery Granny know that his first job was to write film reviews for *The Hindu*. It might have been a couple of decades since he wrote about the likes of Burt Lancaster and Rita Hayworth, but Shankar very well knew his Mila Kunis from an Ashton Kutcher even to the day.

On the dot at the allotted time, Shankar sent a message to Fiery Granny that he was all set to play.

'*How do I start this?*' his message read.

In exchange, he received an invite to play a round of Movies: General with Fiery Granny. For the next twenty minutes, the two sparred at each other like veteran combatants fighting for their respective lands on opposing sides of World War III.

There was subterfuge, confrontation and bitter rancour as, question after question, Fiery Granny and Dr Cool kept their fingers busy, falling back on every ounce of what their memory could recall about films. At the end of four rounds, each had won two rounds, and in the fifth round, Dr Cool had edged past Fiery Granny with 115 points versus 85 points.

The last question, however, had double points. So, technically while Shankar had a solid lead, he could potentially lose if Fiery Granny gave the right answer and bagged 40 points straight up. On the other hand, all Shankar had to do was answer in time to get 11 points or more. This meant that even if Fiery Granny got a clean home run of 40 points, with his existing lead of 30 points, Shankar's 11 points on this question would be just enough to nudge past her.

The dice was loaded, one would have to say, in favour of Dr Cool.

The last question stared at them:

Which of the following Woody Allen movies did not win an Oscar?

A)   *Interiors*
B)   *Hannah and Her Sisters*
C)   *Annie Hall*
D)   *Mighty Aphrodite*

The clock started ticking down from twenty seconds and Shankar was in a real fix to choose between *Interiors* and *Mighty Aphrodite*. Of course, the whole world knew that *Annie Hall* and *Hannah and Her Sisters* had won Oscars. His first reaction was to go for *Mighty Aphrodite* because a strong voice from his memory told him that *Interiors* was nominated for a whole bunch of Oscars. The probability that *Interiors* would've won was high. Except that *Mighty Aphrodite* was the weakest film of the lot, so it was plausible that it didn't win any Oscar.

The seconds counted down to sixteen. Whatever Shankar wanted to pick as the right answer, he had to make that choice in the next five seconds. He also had no way of finding what Fiery Granny had chosen. His mind said *Interiors* and his heart said *Mighty Aphrodite*.

The seconds went down to thirteen and with frenzy gripping him, Shankar went for *Interiors* and hoped against hope that he had sailed through.

The quiz closed with a gentle sound of a 'ting'. It was a good sound. It meant his answer was right. Shankar's eyes darted towards the top right. If she had got it wrong, he was through.

But she got it right too. In fact, she bagged the full bonus for it because she answered it in the shortest possible time. That got Fiery Granny a full forty points. And that meant that Shankar had to score a minimum of eleven points. He looked up at his score. He had scored ten.

It was a tie.

Shankar banged the table on which the iPad was kept. It thudded on to the floor. When he picked it up, he saw a thin crack on the screen. But he couldn't care less.

'Chicken, my foot! I almost had her. Bloody *Interiors*. Couldn't come to me earlier, could it?' Shankar muttered under his breath.

He heard another 'ting' on the iPad. It was a message from Fiery Granny.

'*You did well, champ.*'

Shankar wasn't expecting this. It helped calm his raging nerves. And then a string of messages thereafter almost shook his world.

'*Coffee tomorrow?*'

'*Sorry, I assumed that you are from Bengaluru too.*'

'*Not that I am chickening out of this. But, hey, no pressure.*'

For the next five minutes, Shankar paced up and down his room not knowing what would be an apt response. If anything, Fiery Granny turned out to be quite graceful. And forward thinking.

Shankar looked up his picture in the profile and gave himself some credit for the perfectly greying hair combed back, which might have melted this Granny.

He composed himself and went all over the messages again. He had run out of quiz partners at the Quiz Club events anyway. Maybe, this could be the beginning of a beautiful friendship. He smiled to himself thinking of that famous line from *Casablanca*.

Suddenly, this iPad had opened up a world of opportunities. He put the device back up on the table and framed his reply.

'*Thanks, champ. You were great too.*'

'*Yes, I am from Bengaluru and will be happy to come down to wherever you are for that coffee or whatever your vice maybe.*'

He heard back from her.

'*Starbucks, Koramangala, Saturday, 8 p.m. I know how you look from your profile picture here. I will find you in the coffee shop if you put yourself up to this.*'

'*Of course, I will,*' pat came the reply.

On the eve of the meeting, Shankar dragged Damodar along to buy himself a crisp new shirt and paired it with an old blue denim. He had once overheard Navya speak to someone over the phone, 'You can never go wrong with a blue denim and a white shirt.' And God knows that Shankar didn't want to go wrong with this.

At 8 p.m., Shankar seated himself at a corner table in Starbucks and awaited his date for the evening.

At 8.15 p.m., a young lady member of the staff approached him and asked if he wanted anything.

Shankar felt uncomfortable to order anything here. It was his first time in this fancy coffee shop. He politely declined and said that he was waiting for someone.

'It wouldn't be a Fiery Granny, I suppose,' she said.

'Sorry, I had to close some bills before ending my shift for the day,' she continued.

Shankar took a moment to realize that Fiery Granny was this little kid strutting around in the café as a waiting staff. He let that sink in, perhaps slightly disappointed that his date for the evening wasn't a sultry grandmother.

But she had a delectable smile and eyes darker than chocolate. 'Sorry to disappoint you, but this is me. I just had to meet someone who came so close to beating me on Quiz-Up. I suppose you were expecting a dignified lady your age, but I have been known to be a prodigy at quizzing. Especially when it comes to films.'

Shankar absorbed all the news coming his way and extended his hand, 'I am delighted to meet you, Fiery Granny. May I take the liberty of saying that you remind me of my granddaughter? What's your name, young lady?'

'You absolutely may,' she said. 'I have been searching for quizzing partners all year long and everyone seems a little short of my standards. My name is Avantika. Can I take you as my partner for Quizzing Association's round-up next week? They have a special round on films.'

'You absolutely may,' a delighted Dr Cool retorted.

I have extensively used Quiz-Up and pride myself on a winning track record in the Movies: General section of the app. Last year, I lost five times in a row to a lady from Austin, Texas. When I gave up and finally congratulated her on her winning streak, we started chatting on the app. That's when I found out, she was fourteen.

Or so she said. We'll never know.

Smart Lass and Daft Watch

'Hey, watch it,' said the sassy metallic black smartwatch to the clunky silver HMT watch.

They were settled right next to each other on two economy class seats, each caressing the wrists of their respective men. The younger man, Jason, was assiduously at work on his laptop. One by one, he was going through all the mails that he had labelled as important from the day before. As a busy hotelier, he could accomplish a lot of work during these flights. The other older gentleman was absorbed in the sports pages of the *New Indian Express*. They were both oblivious to the simmering tension between their respective watches.

It wasn't HMT's fault though. Daft Watch just happened to occupy more elbow room on the common armrest between the economy seats on that flight between Bengaluru and Mumbai.

'I am sorry,' Daft Watch yawned in response. 'I haven't shed any weight in the last five decades I guess.'

'I am surprised you are even alive,' said Smart Lass.

'Me too. I thought I could just live the rest of my life sleeping. I was suddenly yanked out of a trunk this morning. I don't even know where I am going,' Daft Watch said disinterestedly.

'You're going to Mumbai, you idiot. I see on my GPS that's where we are tracking towards.'

'Oh, is it? That's where Damodar's daughter stays. Maybe he is going to meet her. What about you?'

'I have meetings that my man has scheduled. Important meetings all day long. It's just another day in the office to be honest. We have big deals to sign. I know his calendar only too well.'

'Really, what is this schedule?' Daft Watch was yet to fully wake up.

'We land. An Uber comes up. He makes calls on the way to the meeting, then he orders a protein-rich breakfast through his secretary, Stella, and then I remind him every now and then about his next meeting. Occasionally, he checks how many steps he has taken through the day and multiple other things. Too many things to detail. Oops, wait a second.'

'What happened?'

'Quiet,' Smart Lass said, going all serious.

Smart Lass hushed him and lifted her eyes with complete attention on her master and commander, Jason. Just then, an air hostess approached the aisle to take orders for tea and coffee.

'Ooh, I see. He likes her. He is getting excited.'

'Well, how do you know that?'

'His heartbeat. I keep a track of his heartbeat every second. I know exactly when his BPM rises.'

'What's that?'

'Beats per minute, you dunce. Where were you living all these years?'

'I don't remember the last time I was on Damodar's wrist. You could say I have been under the rock. He took me out today from that trunk under his bed. What else has changed in the last twenty years? I see the planes are pretty much the same with one armrest in between. Why couldn't they change this all these years?' Daft Watch slurred. He could barely get the words out of his mouth.

'Look, it's been only a year since I was born. I have what you call a fast life. I get replaced every two years. I don't know what's been going on for the last twenty years, but I'll tell you this. I ain't seen a thing as clunky as you on anyone's wrist in the last year I have been around. I can't make any Yo Momma So Fat jokes on you because you are the Fat Momma.'

'So, you live for only one more year?'

'Yeah, that's it, baby. And then I get an upgrade, a Version 3.0, if you will. Inevitably we become more powerful and thinner as the years progress.'

'Yeah, about that—I wanted to check with you. I am seeing all petite things on everyone's wrist now. What's wrong with people?'

'They have taste and class now, sir! That's what's wrong with people now. You don't fit in here any more. You should go back to dying.'

'There was a time when men liked their women, wine and watches full-bodied. Not any more, I guess,' Daft Watch rued.

'I don't know what you are talking about, bruh.'

'What's bruh?'

'Never mind. Look, I am gonna get a power nap, okay. Could you find someone else to talk to?'

'Umm . . . there used to be a time when thick, broad watches like us used to be in vogue. It was mad, the nineties, I tell you. Bappi Lahiri used to be our brand ambassador. He was so good. You heard of him?'

'No. No clue. Look, I wanna get some sleep here before the flight lands in another twenty minutes. Mind if you just shut your trap?'

HMT felt a little humiliated. No one had ever spoken to him like that, and he wasn't going to let this newborn lass take him for granted. He tried to speak up coherently. 'You don't get to talk to me like that. Where are you getting all that attitude from?'

'Hey, you are out of line now, okay? First, you take up so much space on the armrest. Then I educate you on this new age we are living in. Now, all I ask for is twenty minutes of peace. Is that too much to ask?'

'Yeah, well, that lesson was invaluable. You saved my life.'

'Hey, was that sarcasm? I can't tell now. Not until my next 3.0 version is out anyway. But no more talking,' Smart Lass said and closed her eyes.

Before Daft Watch could respond, Smart Lass emanated a series of blinking signals along with short quick beeps. 'Hey, what's that? Why are you making that sound?' Daft Watch asked her, concerned.

Smart Lass had nothing to say except those beeps. It woke up Jason, who had shut down his laptop and was trying to get a quick nap before the flight landed. Jason touched her crown and adjusted it a couple of times. The beeping didn't stop.

'Hey, Smart Lass, why do you have these hiccups? Need some water?'

Smart Lass was gasping. 'It's a virus attack. I can't breathe.'

'Virus attack? What is that? Like aliens coming down? Do I need to be worried?' Daft Watch rolled his eyes trying to stay awake and looked around for signals of invasion from aliens.

'Oh no! I think I am going to have to shutdown. Jason, please pull a normal shutdown, please,' Smart Lass breathed heavily.

Jason, however, couldn't be less bothered. 'Not again, you piece of crap. Why do you hang up on me so much?'

HMT was aghast. Was this the new way watch owners spoke to their beloved timepieces that stayed so close to their human pulse?

'Can I help, Smart Lass? Is there anything I can do? Just say it.'

Her screen had faded to black. Without a word, she was gone.

'I am going to have to give her to Stella,' Jason murmured, closed his eyes and rested his head against his seat.

HMT, a little unnerved with the events of the past five minutes, stayed up for the rest of the flight, hot and bothered.

Once the flight landed, Jason followed the very schedule that Smart Lass had effectively pinned down to every detail. Uber, breakfast, meeting. She missed one tiny thing before his meeting commenced.

'Stella, thanks for that flight booking. Saved me last minute. My Apple watch ran out of juice again. Can you just discard it someplace environment-friendly? Thank you.'

'Do you want me to place you on a waitlist for Version 3.0?' a dutiful Stella inquired.

'No, don't. In fact, on the plane today, I had a neighbour who was wearing this really sturdy piece. Looked timeless. It was silver, had a real man's feel to it. Look out for one like that for me, will you?'

Meanwhile, Damodar headed straight to the Oberoi Hotel where his estranged daughter was celebrating his grandchild Ayan's eighteenth birthday.

'Here's something for you, Ayan. I had it on when you were born and kept it for this day. It's pudgier than what kids wear these days, but it will always keep time and never conk off. I hope it reminds you of your grandfather, much after I am gone. Just the way it reminded me of mine.'

As Daft Watch changed hands, he thought of Smart Lass and hoped she was okay.

Short and Tweet

It took Sonam Carvalho a good decade to build a name for herself as *Cosmopolitan's* features editor. Yet most people still recognized her as the has-been Bollywood diva. Not that she had had a long career. After delivering two monster hits in the mid-nineties, Sonam decided it wasn't for her. The fact that she married soon after and had a child in haste didn't help her cause either.

When her husband divorced her, she promptly left Mumbai with her three-year-old daughter. She felt betrayed by the city that promised to offer her so much and yet delivered little in terms of happiness. When she came back to her home town—Bengaluru—in 2004, she started a blog called Trials of Tinsel Town that gradually amassed enough readers to catch the attention of *Cosmopolitan*. An erratic writing affair soon turned into a fortnightly column.

By the summer of 2016, her daughter, Kavya, now fifteen, had grown up to be the quintessential bright millennial. Academically, she aced her classes, learnt to play the guitar and was vying for a place in the national U-16 basketball team. And as far as Sonam could tell, she didn't miss a father figure.

In the same time, Sonam had established herself as an observant, witty and sensitive writer. The new career Sonam had carved out for herself helped to wean her off the financial dependence on her ex-husband, Jason.

'No, you needn't send in money any more. I request you,' she told him over the phone.

Jason, a busy hotelier, wanted to be around to help Kavya. He could never give them time flitting across time zones in the US and India, managing a new-age upmarket hotel chain called Sukoon.

'How else can I be a part of her life?' Jason demurred.

'I don't know now. I will tell you in case she decides to go to the US for higher studies. I sure won't be able to afford that,' a candid Sonam confessed.

What she also wanted to say was that if Jason ever decided to come back and make Bengaluru his home, it would have meant a lot to Sonam. But she held back. The truth was that all her friends in Bengaluru had a male companion and sometimes Sonam missed having a partner by her side.

She did try Tinder once to get a date for a wedding in the extended family but that didn't amount to much. Kids half her age propositioned straight up to sleep with her. One particularly adventurous businessman offered her Rs 50,000 for a night. That was the final straw that led to an uninstall.

But there was an unlikely app that came to Sonam's rescue. Kavya had set up a Twitter profile for her mother, which in a matter of a year grew to garner over 25,000 followers. It was just a question of time before she became an independent authoritative voice for liberal thinking. Women's empowerment, in particular, was something she was committed to drive awareness for. She often gave her time to NGOs like Nanhi Kali to shoot promos without expecting anything in return. Being with young women and supporting their education became second nature to her.

As her social standing grew with her support for issues of women's empowerment, she was even courted by TV channels to be on prime-time news hour debates. Sonam, now realizing that she had a relevant audience she could cater to, turned her attention to a self-help book for single mothers. Though the book didn't set the bookstores on fire, her publishers just about recovered all the associated costs.

Her followers on Twitter continued to grow as she voiced her opinion without fear. Soon, consumer brands approached her to promote all things from cornflakes to jewellery. The more she refused to stay away from blatant commercial promotions, the more her credibility grew. Once in a while, she accepted a deal to promote a brand's products. It only helped open more doors for her.

Before one knew, Twitter became a unique triage of commerce, dialogue and dating for Sonam. All she needed as a filtering tool was the profile description of any man who commented with decent grammar on her tweets. If the opposite party came up with a 'Let's catch up' over direct messages, Sonam would happily exchange numbers on Twitter. The intelligentsia on Twitter comprised them all—liberals, left liberals and the righteous right. A harmless coffee or a beer often yielded interesting company and conversation.

No one had swept her off her feet yet, but the potential of Twitter for dating pleasantly surprised her. Despite moving on miles away from her life in Mumbai, both literally and figuratively, one thing still bugged her. Most people still spoke of her as a former actress and not so much as a columnist or an author.

In public places like shopping malls, young and middle-aged men and women would want to click pictures with her because, as she would often overhear, 'she used to be quite hot in her younger days' or because 'she acted with yesteryear star Romil Kapoor in a couple of films'.

Couldn't people give her credit for raising her child independently and carving a new successful career out of it? Faceless men and women who trolled her endlessly on different social media channels only aggravated her belief.

One such evening, when yet another troll referred to her as Romil Kapoor's keep, a pleasant distraction cropped up on Twitter.

His name was Rishaad Mehta. For his self-confessed age of forty-six, he looked incredibly in shape in the profile picture, but it was his terse profile description that caught Sonam's eye.

Present day chef, ex-CIA. Don't ask how. But would like to tell you why.

He had just retweeted her new blog with a comment that read thus:

This is the kind of intelligent writing that India so largely deserves but rarely gets.

She responded immediately to that comment with a: '*Thank you. That's the kind of praise we hope for on Twitter but rarely get.*'

During the next five minutes, they both followed each other, and a snappy conversation ensued on direct messages. Phone numbers were exchanged and Sonam found herself drawn into Rishaad's fascinating two worlds that had nothing to do with each other. And every new conversation with him led to something even more unfathomable.

Rishaad was equally attracted to Sonam. He had never seen any of her films and liberally pulled her leg about her starring in Bollywood movies of the nineties. He called that era the dark ages that wouldn't light up even if you placed the sun right next to it.

The conversation was unstoppable. And when they were not talking, they snooped around each other's photographs on Facebook. Soon, the snooping led to a coffee and a subsequent dinner. The chemistry was palpable and sparks flew even without any physical expression whatsoever.

To allow the flying sparks to garner some breathing space, Sonam once called him over to her apartment for dinner. It also tied in well because Kavya was off to the airport that evening to fly to Chennai for her basketball trials the next morning.

Sonam spent a while deciding her attire for the evening. She wished she had spent that time meeting the deadline for an article commissioned by *Cosmopolitan*. But the dress was important, very important. It had to be casual but not flippant. It had to invite but not with open arms. It had to merely tease, not suggest.

And while she was still in her pajamas, the doorbell rang. Her heart soared with expectation, but it was the cook for the evening whom she dismissed in a huff.

Rishaad had promised to take over the chef's mantle for the evening. Sonam eventually settled on a little yellow dress that she had also worn for one of her book launch events.

The bell rang again at 7.30 p.m. She once again checked the setting of her living room that was gently bathed in yellow lights, took a deep breath and opened the door. Rishaad was there with a bottle of wine, immaculate in a blue linen jacket.

Their eyes met and they greeted each other. He kept the bottle of wine on a side table and leaned in to kiss her on the cheek by way of a warm greeting.

And before they knew it, their lips had invaded each other's. Sonam couldn't remember the last time she had flung herself into someone else's arms with such abandon. Rishaad's hands, which at the beginning of this long kiss had adoringly cupped her face, were now wandering all over Sonam's lithe body.

She felt a series of gentle pushes that had now laid her on the grey couch in the centre of the living room. The Tchaikovsky mix she played on her iPhone could barely be heard now because overtaking everything else were their excited gasps.

Five minutes later, they were both naked and very pleased with the choice they had made to get this sexual tension out of the way. The wild lovemaking session was in its final throes when, with a little creak of the door, in walked Kavya with her travel bag.

The primal reactions that Rishaad and Sonam had uncorked for each other made them forget that the door had been left ajar.

When Sonam saw her daughter, the first image that flashed before her eyes was from when she had held Kavya in her arms for the very first time. And then she felt an utter burst of misery within her lungs. It was not the kind of pain that you could mitigate by crying or wailing. It was much worse.

But Kavya wasn't bothered. She looked away and tiptoed into her room.

Rishaad collected himself and left after telling Sonam that he would call again.

Sonam locked herself in her bedroom. She had a million thoughts racing through her mind. She felt like her head would explode any moment with this frenzied after-party her nerve cells seemed to be hosting in her brain.

She decided to complete the *Cosmopolitan* article she was supposed to submit.

Ten minutes later, Sonam received a text on her cell from her daughter.

'*I am sorry, Mama, I should've knocked.*'

It pleased Sonam's heart no end to see this bit of maturity from Kavya.

'*It's all right, beta. I could've also closed the door. :-)*'

'*You fine, right? Come out na.*'

Not even the separation from her husband or the birth of her child had overwhelmed her so much. She wiped a tear off and replied. '*Finishing up an article, beta, will be out in half an hour.*'

'*All right. I am waiting for dinner. Oh, we don't have to go to Chennai this week. Some major floods.*'

Sonam took less than an hour to complete the piece and knowing that Kavya was waiting for her, she decided to step out of her room.

The teenager was sprawled on the sofa, switching channels. When she heard Sonam's door click open, Kavya declared, 'Feel like some Chinese, Mama.'

The rest of the evening was as normal as any other day.

Kavya spoke about her team and how she thought her chances stacked up against the other girls. She felt her rebounds in the offensive court lent her a slight advantage. Sonam spoke about how her publisher was pushing her to write another book, but she didn't think she had enough in the armoury any more.

They both had a glass of the wine that Rishaad had brought and bid each other goodnight.

Sonam locked her door and felt a huge sense of gratitude and relief. She turned to her cellphone. There wasn't any message or call from Rishaad. But Sonam felt incredibly awake. She was itching to tell the world about what just happened but she couldn't, so she decided to do what she did best: write.

She wrote of how single mothers are often said to be selfish in not giving their children a fatherly figure but how this incident proved that that was an urban myth. It was all about the upbringing you gave to your children.

Every second of the last couple of hours was so fleshed out in front of her, that in a single sitting she swiftly pared it all out in two pages.

And then at 2.30 a.m., she emailed her *Cosmopolitan* editor this two-pager instead of the article she was supposed to send.

As usual, her editor sent in a standard response: 'This is great!' in reply the next morning.

The hangover of last evening hadn't yet gone out of her head, so Sonam's first tweet the next morning was: *Terrible day yesterday, saved by my fifteen-year-old angel.*

Another hour later, her phone kept pinging more than usual. Even some of the one-word attacks those regular trolls often used grew harsher.

'Slut'

'Bitch needs it badly!'

And then the specificity of one message from a menial gave Sonam a jolt in the head.

'*Call me over. We can do it on the couch and lock the door this time.*'

It didn't take long for Sonam to figure out what had happened. She called her editor.

'Sam, that is not the story I meant to send.'

'What are you talking about! It's great. People are loving it.'

'Sam, please take it down. I can't have this going everywhere.'

'What do you mean?'

'I will explain, but can you please take it down.'

Sonam described her side of the story. Sam pulled the story off the *Cosmopolitan* website, but by now the article had mushroomed on a lot of aggregator sites.

Despite the piece not being available on *Cosmopolitan* any more, people who were still able to access the story from their Internet cookies, copy-pasted it and put it up elsewhere.

In between, Kavya called Sonam.

'Do you have any clue about what my friends are talking about? Why can't you keep your bedroom stories confined to yourself? I didn't need your public endorsement.'

The damage was done. Sonam tried to explain and apologized, but Kavya was in no mood to listen.

By noon, the story was carried by all the popular content aggregator sites. Some called it funny. Some expressed disgust and some couldn't care much and moved on to the next clickbait.

Sonam got a long-awaited message from Rishaad, about whom she had forgotten since the madness began in the morning. *'You are a crazy woman! I am blocking you forever . . .'*

Kavya got home at 3 p.m. and Sonam sat her down to talk about how this was an honest mistake. She urged Kavya to be patient with her, and that she was regretting this no end, and that despite hers and *Cosmopolitan's* best efforts, the article couldn't be stopped from mushrooming further.

At 6 p.m. that evening, Sonam had a message from Jason. *'Listen, it's okay. It will be fine. Trust me it will. If you need to talk, let me know.'*

Sonam had engaged one of *Cosmopolitan*'s digital partners to filter and wash up the Internet as frequently as possible. A legal team was also helping her put together a notice for any sites that would carry the story, to be warned that the content was original and couldn't be distributed freely on the Internet.

Sonam was waiting for an update from *Cosmopolitan*. At 7.30 p.m., Sam called.

'I need to be sure that you still want us to go ahead with de-barring the article from appearing after what's happened,' Sam said.

'Yeah, I am sure,' Sonam replied.

Sam sighed. 'But you should at least tweet Sheryl and Mark back.'

'Sorry, who?'

'What do you mean who? Haven't you seen?'

'I have no clue what you're talking about,' Sonam was getting impatient.

'Sheryl Sandberg and Mark Zuckerberg, you idiot. They have called your story the most honest piece of writing that they almost wished came out from the hearts of single working mothers in the Silicon Valley. Oh wait, I need to be precise here. Sheryl tweeted that and Mark posted it on Facebook. The business news channels are going nuts about it.'

Sonam disconnected the phone and went to her Twitter profile. Hundreds of people she didn't know were congratulating her on the article. Sam sent her a few screenshots of laudatory messages he received from his peers in other publications. Meanwhile, some smart-ass tagged Kavya, commending her on her wisdom as a teenager.

While this madness was going on, a leading prime-time TV presenter decided to host a Facebook Live event for the first time, describing Sonam Carvalho as a brutally honest, independent, caring mother and the best columnist he had ever known. He also called Sonam one of their own because she had come in for one of the channel's panel discussions last year.

A stunned Kavya came into the living room and hugged Sonam. She sobbed. 'You are the best writer ever. Never ever let me tell you what to write.'

Sonam sunk into the same couch that had led to this circus and logged in to Twitter.

She then turned on the TV and put it on mute.

The news tickers said, 'Indian *Cosmopolitan* writer bares heart and raises hope for single mothers worldwide.'

The word 'writer' gleamed back at her more than any of the others.

Shop Now

Shashank Raman was addicted to online shopping. It occupied every minute of his waking hours and consumed him in his sleep. He had gone past the mainstream digs of Banjara Hills and Jubilee Hills of Hyderabad. For him, the new wave in the online shopping scenario in India was represented by the likes of boutique dwellings such as Bombay Shirt Company and Gentleman's Corner.

A minor impediment in his online shopping addiction was that Shashank was still a final year engineering student at IIIT, Hyderabad, with no prospect of an independent income on the anvil. His father, a physics professor at the same university, had given Shashank a free rein on his career choices, but Shashank couldn't care less. For him, engineering was merely a stepping stone before he joined the fashion industry. His mother, separated from his father, didn't have much to say about it. When Shashank spoke to her, she appeared more concerned about the alimony from her father being delayed the last couple of months.

'I will speak to dad about it,' Shashank comforted her.

'He is still sleeping around with those whores from his university, isn't he?' she snarled.

Shashank remained quiet.

Listening to his mother convinced him that it was she who was unreasonable. And when he spent time listening to his father, he was convinced of the contrary.

To get away from these unpleasant exchanges since his parents' separation three years ago, Shashank immersed himself in online shopping. The neatly organized stacks of gleaming footwear and apparel, at the command of his scroll, came in handy to get away from the bitterness his parents harboured for each other. Slowly and steadily, Shashank found all his weekly pocket money diverted to these online indulgences. While most students his age took to pornography on campus to relieve their stress, Shashank relied on online shopping.

He had also found a way around to order new shirts, belts, jackets and what-not without spending much. It pertained to the loophole in the return policy on these sites. Almost all the shopping sites had at least a seven-day return policy.

This meant that Shashank could order a new set of clothes on a Tuesday, which would invariably be delivered at his home in Gulshan Colony by Friday. He would wear these clothes for the next few days and then return them to the website within a week citing fit, quality or design concerns. For some websites, he had to keep the shopping tags on, while others were a lot more generous. Once the original merchandise reached the website's warehouse, his money would be refunded to his credit card.

Once every couple of months, Shashank also made sure that he bought something he liked from the sites whose merchandise he was frequently returning. That established him as a genuine buyer on these platforms and helped him evade a deviant shopper red-flag that smart-shopping platforms were quick to raise.

Shashank's reliance on this sly modus operandi escalated when his father saw his credit card bill and discovered a slew of shopping sites mentioned on it. He was incensed that Shashank was spending every cent of the Rs 10,000 he received every month on clothes.

'This money was for you so that you learn to spend it on things that are important for your education. Not for this ghastly purpose you are putting it to,' he growled and promptly stopped Shashank's monthly allowance.

The economic sanction that his father placed on Shashank upset him. But he continued with his usual mode of ordering-for-the-sake-of-returning style of purchases with increased fervour. His frequent orders and returns made him a familiar figure with the delivery boys of his neighbourhood. Soon, he became friends with one of the delivery boys—twenty-year-old Yousuf Anis.

Yousuf offered to introduce Shashank to the warehouse manager at Myntra, who was always happy to employ more delivery boys.

'I know the warehouse manager well. You won't even have to prepare a résumé for a job. And if you get hired, I will make an extra Rs 1000 as referral bonus,' Yousuf added.

'I will let you know. I want to get my final exams out of the way. I will then be able to devote more time to make these deliveries,' Shashank informed him.

This was true. Shashank's final year project on applications of machine learning in primary education was a daunting affair.

Shashank wasn't exactly a gifted student, but he was happy to put in the hours required to earn a respectable grade. To be a student in the same college that your father teaches in carried its own pall of expectations. This added pressure of the final project meant spending more time on the laptop.

It also meant that he went a little further in his online shopping invasions in the month of March.

One day during his final month at college, Aalia, a tall damsel and the daughter of a famed beer brewing family, who sat next to Shashank in an elective class, had something to ask him.

'Shashank, I never see you repeat your clothes. Am I wrong, or am I just imagining that you have an unending wardrobe?'

Aalia, the angelic but high-flying diva in their college, who had set many a young man's heart aflutter, was never known to initiate conversations.

Coming from a family of means, she was known not just for her lineage but also for leading her metallurgy class. She was a shy girl who spoke rarely, but when she did, she had everyone rapt. She never dated anyone and word had got around that she probably didn't deem anyone good enough to match her stature. The truth was that no one had caught her eye until now.

Shashank, who had nursed a crush on her for a long time, saw an opening in her question that could potentially open doors to a friendship, if nothing else. He wasn't going to squander it.

'Yes, I like experimenting with my clothes,' he replied.

Aalia liked men with a good taste in clothes. After that class, one question led to another, and later that evening they went out and had a long chat over several home brews at Belgium Beer House, the veritable treasure of a beer house that Aalia suggested.

Aalia, too, had a weakness for shopping. That provided another window of conversation between the two. Unknown to

Shashank, Aalia, under the pseudonym Girlwithcoloursgalore, ran a fashion blog which among other things had also been featured in *Cosmopolitan India*.

'What are you wearing for the farewell dinner next month? I really want to know,' she asked Shashank with her dreamy blue eyes.

Shashank had an eye on an expensive grey suit from Gentleman's Corner that he had saved under the Wishlist section on the site. He showed it to Aalia on his phone.

She admired it in a way only a fashionista could and sighed. 'You would look like a million bucks in this. I would love to carry a feature on you on my blog. Could you order it right away? Do they have enough stock?'

'Yeah, it will be done. Now that you approve of it,' Shashank replied with a cheeky smile.

As their evening wore on, Shashank discovered some more delightful things about Aalia. She was an expert baker and an accomplished black belt in karate. That she was sitting across the table from him in their last month of college together was a miracle for Shashank. She had already signed up for her master's at the National Institute of Fashion Technology (What else could a rich heiress of a beer baron do?).

It drizzled that night as Shashank saw her off in a cab. She reminded him once again that he should order the suit soon. 'I will be in Bengaluru to meet Sonam, the *Cosmopolitan* features editor, on the 19th, the day before the farewell dinner. We wanted to discuss in detail the other features I could contribute to the magazine. But I am taking the 1 p.m. return flight from Bengaluru on 20th. I should be in the city by late afternoon. Let's do a candid shoot just between ourselves that evening before the farewell. I will call a photographer friend of mine. His pictures are to die for.'

He kissed her on the cheek before the car sped off.

Why wouldn't Shashank agree to this delightful proposition? All his purchases and returns, those hours he had toiled into the wee hours of the night with only the dim light from the laptop for company, had paid off. He was at the mercy of this beautiful lady's love.

The catch was that since the farewell dinner was four weeks away, Shashank couldn't have risked ordering the suit now. Those websites only operated with a seven-day return policy. He wanted to order the suit only when the final date was closer to the dinner, so that he could simply wear it that night and return it to the website the next morning under their customer-friendly return policy.

In order to do that, Shashank would have to convince his father to let him use his credit card one last time. He thought it best to approach the topic with his father in a couple of weeks.

As the date of the farewell dinner approached and early touches of spring began to graze the air of Hyderabad, Shashank received a mail from his favourite shopping portal— Gentleman's Corner. It said something to the effect of how Shashank was a valued customer but considering his recent purchase history, they were temporarily blocking his account for any further returns. The site still allowed him to purchase anything if he so wished but carried a caveat of no more merchandise returns on the account.

This was a complete shocker for Shashank. He went over his purchase history with his favourite site and realized that one fateful night a couple of weeks ago he had ordered clothes worth over Rs 30,000 from Gentleman's Corner.

Shashank needed these extra pieces of clothing for a series of final year meets that were being organized at the university. He wanted to have a different look for each of them since Aalia was now keenly following his wardrobe selection.

To keep pace with these social appearances, Shashank did what he did best and ordered a consignment of some of the season's latest shirts and jackets and denims and trousers and other accessories to go along with it. Little did he realize while ordering that this would turn out to be a consignment worth Rs 30,000. He recalled seeing that number, but it didn't matter to him at all. It was a tried and tested plan. He was only ordering these to return them in a couple of weeks. And he did return every single one of those clothes. Nothing could've gone wrong.

Except that back at the customer analytics division of Gentleman's Corner, Shashank's expensive purchase popped up as a red flag. Someone from the analytics team took notice of this consumer behaviour and flagged it under what has today come to be known as 'anomaly detection'.

Those sharp nerds took a quick look at his purchase history and arrived at the appropriate conclusion that Shashank was what in their business was known as an 'unsustainable customer'.

This species of customers would inevitably order more than they could chew. The cost of handling their logistics of delivery and return was more than the net profit these specific customers brought to the website. With regard to Shashank, when they delved deeper into his transaction history, it became an easy decision for the team to take. They immediately shut down his returns tab and that precursory warning of a mail found its way into Shashank's inbox.

Shashank was in a fix. In less than two weeks, he was to attend that farewell party along with his evening shoot with Aalia. Since their drink that evening, Aalia had also showed him an off-white designer dress that she had purchased off Myntra. It was expensive but Aalia liked Shashank's sartorial adventures and had proceeded to spend Rs 15,000 on her gown at Shashank's behest.

Shashank had only two choices—either he could buy the suit from Gentleman's Corner and not opt for a return, or forget about that specific suit and look for something similar on other websites.

The first was not a real option because the suit was listed at a hefty Rs 20,000 plus taxes and shipping. His father would never allow Shashank to spend that kind of money. He considered setting up another profile on the website, but without a credit card he was in no position to work around the website. Could he borrow anyone else's credit card? That would be opening a Pandora's box of explanations and justifications. He decided against it.

With his options dwindling, he spent a couple of nights browsing grey suits on all other websites but nothing pleased him about any of those. He wanted the suit he had shown Aalia.

The last resort was to get a suit tailor-made, but the farewell was less than ten days away. And what if he didn't get the exact shade and Aalia recognized the difference? She did a have trained eye for fashion.

He thought of people who could possibly bail him out. Yousuf was the only name that popped up in his mind.

'Listen, I've got myself in a fix. Umm . . . you remember my shopping habit?' he asked Yousuf.

'Yeah, man, sure. You want a job at Myntra?'

'Not exactly a job. Not now at least, but I need to get in touch with Gentleman's Corner. Do you know someone there?'

Yousuf mulled this over and spoke, 'I don't think so, but I will have friends who will know someone. Tell me, what happened?' He sensed a flush of desperation in Shashank's voice.

Shashank explained how he landed himself in this awkward position and subtly inquired if Yousuf had a credit card he could lend. Yousuf mentioned he never kept a credit card.

'I have to wear that suit. I have searched for it across all other websites. I am just not getting the one that I want,' Shashank said, exasperated.

'When do you need this suit? Can't you rent it from someone?' Yousuf asked.

'I don't know anyone who has *that* suit.'

'When do you need it?'

'About a week from now.'

'Let me see if I can do something about it.'

For Shashank, it didn't turn out to be an encouraging call. But Yousuf was looking for someone exactly like Shashank. It so happened that he needed something done and he needed someone who would forget the light of reason in exchange for money.

Yousuf found Shashank in the sticky spot which many young boys in Hyderabad found themselves in after college—kids without employment, looking to make a quick buck.

Yousuf, who hailed from Amannagar, a north-western neighbourhood around Hyderabad, was a promising cricketer during his school days who dreamt of playing for Hyderabad. His father, a Muslim cleric, and his mother were convinced that he would make a good cricketer who could one day even be picked up for the Indian national team.

That dream didn't quite go as planned after Yousuf's father was arrested on account of extremist speeches during a peaceful rally around Amannagar. After repeated attempts to have him released failed, Yousuf had no option but to take up odd jobs to support his family. First he became a newspaper delivery boy. Then a grocer's assistant. Soon he couldn't manage his school and his day jobs and so he dropped out of the former.

Other people in and around the neighbourhood came to offer support to Maryam, Yousuf's mother. Maryam, who saw her life fall apart in less than six months, was clueless about Yousuf's future. That's when a wise, old man from the neighbourhood offered to take Yousuf under his wing.

That man was Salah Ahmet. Salah impressed upon Maryam the need for Yousuf to carve his own future and not for him to depend on the mercies of rich Hyderabadis. What he conveniently left out from his merciful submission to help Yousuf was that he was a ground man for the ISIS in India. Salah was the epitome of danger and destruction for humanity in general.

The first thing Salah did was move Yousuf's mother out of their current home to a larger apartment. Food and other supplies began to be delivered to the house through Salah's connections in Amannagar. In exchange, all Salah asked of Yousuf was to find recruits for his movement. It had been less than six months that Yousuf had been working for Salah, but he had already brought in more than twenty-odd youngsters from in and around Amannagar for evening classes with

Salah's trusted advisers. A glib talker, Yousuf could easily convince the youngsters to get a few seemingly inane errands done in exchange for money.

Salah never told Yousuf the real reason behind this recruitment drive. It was a tacit understanding. Time and again, Salah would ask Yousuf to join his classes, but Yousuf would politely decline. Salah's arguments would often take the high ground that he wanted the youth not to stray into illegal activities but instead work with him in spreading the word of Allah.

'We advise you to do more important things than smoke weed or drink alcohol. One day you will understand it,' Salah opined.

Instead, what used to transpire inside a massive apartment complex that Salah owned was intensive training in the handling of arms and ammunition. Those newly recruited would be expected to carry out attacks in and around India for opposing the ISIS. Initially, Yousuf resisted becoming a part of this drive but seeing how much Salah was helping his mother, he caved in.

One day, when a Hyderabad cop forcibly asked Maryam to take off her hijab, Yousuf decided he had had enough. He agreed to participate in one of the secret missions. His mission was to identify and kill a few heathen passengers on a train between Bangalore and Hyderabad. In fact, the ISIS had green-lighted a slew of missions across Europe and Salah needed an administrative hand for booking hotels and trains for his trainees.

Salah told Yousuf that he needed someone quickly as there were six separate missions. He didn't want to involve his trainees for these bookings. The reason why

Salah needed innocent people unrelated to the operation to do these bookings was because many IP addresses of suspicious neighbourhoods were specifically profiled and tracked by the Interpol and Indian intelligence agencies alike. If these bookings were not done by disparate people who were non-Muslims, their operation could come under the scanner.

Shashank Raman perfectly fit the bill of the kind of guy Salah wanted and the job was nothing special. Just a bunch of train, flight and hotel bookings.

'All you need for this is to be constantly connected to the Internet,' Yousuf called Shashank and explained. 'Every morning, for the next three to four weeks, you will get a mail with names and dates that you need to make bookings for. There could be cancellations and rescheduling, but that's it.'

'Who are these bookings for?'

'Traders. Rich businessmen from countries like Morocco and Turkey who come here every spring and buy expensive jewels from Hyderabad. The firm I work for provides them with the best options for diamonds and pearls and other gems in these cities. We function as their de-facto trusted travel partner to show them around, hence the bookings.' This was the standard decoy handed down from Salah to Yousuf.

'And these booking requests come in every day?'

'More or less. We are planning our calendar for summer right now. It's a busy time. Our most trusted travel agent shut shop last month and the company was soliciting new agents. I honestly don't think it takes anything special to book these names, which is why I recommended your name. They will give you Rs 10,000 for a month of co-ordination. Can you do it?'

'Of course, I can. Thanks a lot, Yousuf. This is a big help. Can they pay me in advance?'

It sounded too simple a job to ignore for Rs 10,000. It would help him get that suit! The money came promptly into Shashank's bank account and the booking requests began to pour in from a specific email address. The passengers, whose scanned copies of passports accompanied every booking request, were of diverse nationalities—Algeria, Syria, Turkey, France and even Switzerland.

Shashank wasn't the only one making travel bookings for terrorists. There were two others in different parts of Telangana. How and when a peace-loving city like Hyderabad transformed itself into a hideous but effective web for such extremist activities was anyone's guess. Little did Shashank know that these bookings were for hardened terrorists with multiple passports travelling within India. Over the next week, Shashank dedicated all the time required for these bookings.

Most mornings, Shashank would get a mail and all he had to do was follow instructions. Sometimes he was asked to do a little research and send back a set of recommendations for flights and hotels. Within hours he would get a reply with the selected options from that email address.

With the money from this odd job, Shashank ordered his suit. There was a minor scare about the specific unit not being in stock, but the customer department cleared it over an e-mail saying they could get the extra inventory in the size required.

Spurred on in anticipation of the possibilities that the new suit would bring, Shashank fulfilled all the requests that came his way in a jiffy. In a millennial's world, he would have been called efficient AF. One day, as he got set to finish his last booking request, he got a call from Yousuf.

'Hey, man, I have one more booking for you for the day.'

'Go ahead, shoot. I'll take notes. Am I not getting a mail for this?'

'No, it's for me with one more passenger. So, I figured I'll call you. It's on the Bangalore to Hyderabad route. No hotel bookings. Just a couple of tickets on the Shatabdi train.'

'Wow! You are going to escort the touring party this time, huh?'

'Yeah, about time.'

This was the trip for which Yousuf had been receiving training for over a month now.

Shashank quickly completed the booking and thanked Yousuf for putting him in touch with the good folks at Aegis Exports, the company on whose behalf Shashank was making the bookings. As soon as Yousuf received the tickets, he called Shashank back.

'Do you want to come with us? It would be a good diversion for you.'

Shashank looked at the dates. It was the eve of the farewell dinner. He politely declined.

In a couple of days, Shashank's suit arrived. Despite all the hurdles, this thing of beauty was worth it. He sent a few pictures of his suit to Aalia. She was delirious with excitement. She had already booked the photographer for their evening shoot on the day of the farewell.

The evening of the farewell party, Shashank was decked in his fashionable grey suit by 2 p.m. After trying to call Aalia a few times, he left a message for her. Having not heard from her, he decided to hop over to Belgium Beer House for a drink before leaving for the university. He didn't ever mind getting to any place early.

The usually quiet Belgium Beer House had its television blaring. It carried the report of an attack on a Shatabdi train by two terrorists. While the reporter gave out details of the attack, it also carried Aalia's picture on one half of the screen. It was she who had bravely overpowered a supposedly novice terrorist who couldn't bring himself to fire a gun at the passengers. His other accomplice was overpowered in the scuffle led by other passengers and handed over to the police, but the novice terrorist, identified as a certain Yousuf, had lost his life.

Shashank could barely comprehend the depravity of what his part-time job entailed. With hands shivering at the thought of what he might have helped accomplish, he logged into his e-mail. It had a mail from Aalia.

'*I am taking a train back from Hyderabad, honey. As soon as I landed, got to know that my meeting with Sonam Carvalho at* Cosmopolitan *had been cancelled because she was dealing with some crisis with the current edition. Had an urge to see you as soon as possible and no prior flights were available so took the last train out at night. Can't wait to see you in that grey suit soon. Love, Aalia. XoXo*'

The Telangana government announced the state's highest civilian honour for Aalia in recognition of her bravery. She had succumbed to her injuries on the way to the hospital.

On the day of her funeral, Shashank looked impeccable in his new grey suit.

Last Seen

'The problem with modern dating is that most people would hang a comment here and a question there for the opposite party to respond to on WhatsApp, without making the effort to talk or meet in person,' the wise-looking gentleman, whom we shall call Bertrand, said to a teenager nursing a drink at Plan B after an apparent breakup over WhatsApp.

'Teenagers don't realize it yet, but this heinous app is sounding the death knell of romance in this world at an alarming pace,' he continued.

'It's cruel. She broke up with me on chat. Our generation deserves better,' the teenager replied.

'You are sagacious,' said Bertrand. 'But let me tell you a story that took place in this very town; it might make you feel a little better.'

It's not easy to woo someone on WhatsApp. Yet, it has invariably become the cradle of flirting on college campuses. Everyone is lured by the ease the darned app offers. Venu was no different. After graduating from IIIT, Hyderabad, he had just joined the 2016 MBA batch at the Loyola School of Business, Chennai. From the very first day, he couldn't take his eyes off Menaka. When on Freshers' Day he noticed her clapping rather generously after his solo performance of the popular song *Tu Hi Re*, he thought the ground to be fertile enough to initiate a WhatsApp conversation.

When Menaka received that joke from Venu about Subramaniam Swamy, she broke into a hearty laugh. But the vexing dilemma that an app like WhatsApp imposes on a fledgling relationship is this: all Menaka replied was, *LOL*.

It was a different matter altogether that the doe-eyed Menaka had received at least six memes from different boys in her class, but she deemed only Venu worthy enough for a reply. 'LOL' was the only expression she could come up with.

Poor Venu, who had sifted through so many jokes before sending this one, was heartbroken. LOL is the least common denominator in a budding relationship. It's a cyanide pill disguised as laughter on a chat, a thoroughbred conversation killer. What could be the best comeback to a LOL? Nothing!

Shakespeare might as well have given Romeo and Juliet a smartphone each at the end of Act 5 and asked them to type LOL, such is the poison contained in those three letters.

And there the relationship could've died. But there was more to that LOL. Menaka went up to her sister Dhara who had come to their parents' home to pack for the honeymoon she was leaving for with her husband, Gopal.

'Dhara, listen to this joke,' Menaka demanded.

'Later, *da*. No time. Gopal is on his way to pick me up,' Dhara replied, pushing her swanky blue frame up the bridge of her nose. Gopal and Dhara had dated for a year after she accepted his proposal. It was only a matter of time before they started planning their honeymoon. And here they were, all set to go to New Delhi.

'Listen *na*, this guy sent me this joke. It's damn funny,' Menaka insisted.

'Okay, shoot.'

'What's the opposite of Subramaniam Swamy?'

'What is it?'

'Give it a try, be a sport.'

'I don't know. Out with it,' Dhara, completely occupied with her packing, couldn't care less.

'Are you ready?'

Menaka waited for a response from Dhara while she flung another old pullover into her suitcase.

'You aren't even interested. You've changed since your marriage.' Menaka walked out of the room in a huff.

Dhara followed her and caught hold of her. 'I am a little short of time, honey, that's why. Okay here's my guess. Opposite of Subramaniam Swamy? I see. Maybe Jayalalithaa?'

'No, silly. It's Subramaniam didn't see me,' Menaka chortled.

That got the sisters laughing for a while. 'Is there anything you want from Delhi?' Dhara asked her sister.

'Nothing for me but I will ask my friend Venu if he would like something,' Menaka said.

She went back to her room and stared at Venu's profile picture. He was tall, his hair was a little frumpy, but he had a Napoleon of a nose and a face that could belong to a ramp— a near-perfect combination of tall, dark and handsome with bad hair. The singing was a bonus.

She wanted to write to him that the joke cracked her sister up. But then she wondered if she would be giving too much leeway to a guy she barely knew.

It would be two more days before classes for the first years at the Loyola School of Business would resume. She looked at the time stamp on his chat.

It said, 'Last seen 11.32 a.m.'

Venu slunk into his beanbag and once again looked at her reply. 'LOL.'

Granted it was not an ingenious, original joke but she could've done better than that. He was going nuts thinking of her. It had only been a month since he knew her, a fellow classmate from his neighbourhood, Saidapet. Both twenty-two and single, as acknowledged by themselves at that Freshers' Day party last week.

Before the celebrations began, the seniors made the first-year batch line-up, asked them to pick up tags of whether they were single or committed and keep them on for the evening. Both Venu and Menaka had picked up badges that read 'single'.

'You sang that song really well,' Menaka told Venu right after his performance.

'I am glad you liked it,' Venu blushed.

'I could be presumptuous here but did you take a picture of mine while I was singing or was it my imagination?'

'No, I did click a few for the college report on Freshers' Day. You might not have realized, but I am in the culture committee.'

'Of course, I know,' Venu back-pedalled. His hopes were dashed because he thought she was taking his pictures for herself.

'Could you please send them to me? My mother would love to see them,' he added.

'Done. What's your number?'

It turned out well eventually. He had her number without coming across as a creep.

Yet right now, all he had from that number he so fervently plotted for was an 'LOL'. Come to think of it, her house was only a ten-minute ride from his place.

Should he ask her for a coffee at Hot Breads in the evening? But it's only been a month since they knew each other. Too soon, he concluded. WhatsApp was safer. But what do you ask over chat? What is the right message to send without coming across as too blunt and thus falling by the wayside?

Also, it had been raining since morning. Who knows what the weather would be like in the evening. He was going to give it a couple of hours. If the rain stopped, he would think about how to frame that message. It would need masterful construction.

A couple of hours later, Menaka picked up the phone again to see if there was any response to her 'LOL' from Venu. *Such a perfectly legitimate response to a good joke*, she thought. Yet, he couldn't come up with a conversation starter? Why should she? The 'last seen' time was now 1.34 p.m.

'If he's on WhatsApp and connected, why can't he ask me something about my day or my plans for the weekend? I have even seen his house. A little coffee at Hot Breads wouldn't hurt. Once the rain clears up, the weather is going to be cool and breezy. Why do all boys have to play so hard to get?' Menaka kept thinking about him and fittingly spent the afternoon in the company of a Nicholas Sparks novella.

When Venu woke up from his siesta, it was 4 p.m. The rain showed no sign of abatement. It occurred to him that going to her place might be a better option than asking her to come out.

He plotted his decision-making on a flowchart on a whiteboard.

- She replied to my message at 11.32 a.m. It's been raining since morning.
- She doesn't have a car, so she couldn't have stepped out. She told me that last week.
- I am dying to see her. I can't go through two more days without seeing her.
- If I visit her place, maybe bring a book or something, I can't be doing anything wrong.
- She stays with her mother. Mothers are normally sweet. I can have a cup of tea with them and come back home.

Meanwhile, hearing that familiar swoosh of an incoming message, Menaka rushed to her phone. She hoped it was from Venu. It wasn't. It was Dhara. She and Gopal had reached the airport. A few flights were cancelled, but the Delhi flight was on schedule.

She messaged Menaka that they were all set to take off. She also told her to get the domestic help to wash Gopal's Honda CR-V every alternate day. Since Gopal was running late, he didn't want to go back to keep the car at his apartment. It was a temporary arrangement. Dhara and Gopal stayed at another end of the city but it was closer to get to the airport from Dhara's family home, hence Gopal thought it best to leave the car with Menaka and her mother.

But this message from Dhara interested her. She suddenly had a car at her disposal. She could swing by Venu's place for coffee. It was only a few blocks away.

If Menaka asked permission from her mother, it could turn into a slug fest. She was desperate to see him. This was the first time Venu had messaged her directly outside of their group. She wanted to tell him in person what a funny joke it was. With a decision made, she turned on the ignition of her brother-in-law's CR-V and set off from her house on 12th Avenue towards Venu's house in Raghava Colony—a trifle matter of a few blocks.

Six blocks ahead, Venu concluded that there was no point asking if he should come over. They had briefly spoken about Jim Collins' *Good to Great* as being a great read and he had that book with him. He had even told her that he would bring it for her someday to college. The alibi was watertight. It would go thus: 'I was just passing by so thought of dropping this. I have read it. Return it whenever you feel like.' He drooled over the thought.

There was no point calling her in advance to take time and all that. That would make it seem very serious. He picked up the book and set off for her house in his rickety old Maruti Zen.

As soon as Venu stepped out on 1st Street in Raghava Colony, he couldn't believe what hit him. The Nagathamman Koil Main Road was flooded in knee-deep water. A handful of men were crossing the road very carefully and no other cars were around. All he had to do was drive straight for five minutes on this main road and take a right on 12th Avenue. But it seemed an impossible task to undertake. Such was the fury of the rain.

Venu tried to turn his car around but it was a little too late to go back. The engine just wouldn't crank up enough to move ahead or even turn. He pressed the accelerator hard.

The engine roared all right but there was an underlying sense of surrender. Soon, it spluttered into silence.

There was only one way out from here. He had to get out of the car and walk back home. Desperate, he felt like calling a friend and reached out for his phone in his pocket.

Normally, he would simply place his phone in his right pocket but was it possible that it had slipped out under the seat today? He looked but his phone was nowhere to be found. In his excitement to carry the book for Menaka, he had forgotten it at home.

He started the engine again. A whimper is all he got. It was time to step out in the water. But his side of the door was stuck. Murphy's Law was having a field day with Venu. He reached out for the other doors. None of them responded.

A few blocks away, Menaka was taken aback with the brute force of water that thudded into her car when she passed the KFC outlet on 12th Avenue. She pondered about going back, but the SUV was a good beast to have on your side. It was barely knee-deep on her side of the street. Besides, she had enough practice with this vehicle to trust herself around it. She carefully navigated the CR-V for the next five minutes and reached Nagathamman Koil Main Road where Venu's car was stuck.

She plodded along steadily on 1st gear. She caught sight of a couple of men wading through the water.

Venu—who could only see this one car from the other end—banged the windows for help. The car was headed in his direction. Perhaps, it was his only hope to get out of this alive. Just then he saw who was driving the CR-V.

From inside his Zen, he screamed her name.

Menaka, on the other hand, was so focused on getting to his house that she didn't hear a thing. She turned into Venu's street and parked her car in front of his house. Drenched in the merciless rain, she ran inside the open gates up to his door and rang the bell.

She waited for a few minutes before giving it another ring.

She got back into the car and called him. She went to WhatsApp. Venu's last seen stamp was 4:04 p.m.

The rain pounded hard on her car. She thought it best to turn back. On her way back, she risked a shortcut. It was marginally better than the main road.

The moment Menaka got home, she looked at her phone. There was still no call or message from Venu.

A kind couple, also in an SUV, who were passing by Nagathamman Koil Road ten minutes later, spotted a lean boy with a panic-stricken face in a Zen. While her husband stopped the car, the lady stepped out, held her expensive sari a little above her knees, and approached the car. She used her hair clip to help open his door. They were also kind enough to drop him home.

Venu clutched the book tightly on his way home. While the old couple sought to make idle conversation, all Venu could think about was his doomed Zen that by now had water all the way up to its windows. He didn't even have insurance for the car.

Venu came home and went straight to his mobile phone. He didn't bother to see if he had missed any calls. He went straight to WhatsApp. The last seen stamp on Menaka's chat was 4.34 p.m. The last message from her was still LoL.

He replied with rage writ all over him. *'I almost died, thanks to you, bitch.'* And with that he promptly uninstalled the app.

From thereon, Menaka sent a flurry of messages that went undelivered. The college was closed for the next five days due to the floods that had paralysed the city.

When college reopened, they never spoke again.

Welcome Home

Gopal and Dhara were the quintessential New Age couple. That they were from Chennai didn't entirely exclude them from trying to be 'millennial cool'. They earned so that they could spend. While Gopal plied his trade as an export manager for a textile company, Dhara was an accountant with one of Chennai's leading chit funds.

They had spent a considerable amount of time since their dating days to plan their honeymoon. Married at twenty-six and having saved for a year, they had just about amassed enough to take a much-desired trip to north India. Like true digital natives, they read about all the best hotels, restaurants and tourist sights on various recommendation engines and settled upon New Delhi.

At each of the places, they booked their Airbnbs well in advance. After checking into Facebook and letting the world know that they were off from Chennai Airport on a day of torrential downpour, they landed in New Delhi after an energy-sapping flight in the world-class economy buckets of Air India.

A sixty-minute ride from the airport brought them to Greater Kailash-2. Their first impression of New Delhi was that this vast city had better roads than Chennai.

Dhara, who had led all the accommodation bookings, informed their host Debbie Malhotra that they were en route. Cheerful Debbie said their room was all set and they could knock on her apartment number 2B for the keys. The building name would be etched against the wall, 'It reads Green Sanctum Apartments,' Debbie said.

Once the cab driver arrived at the destination and got their two large bags out of the boot of the car, he demanded his tip with a face that frowned rather munificently.

Gopal and Dhara looked at the building in front of them. It was grey and looked newly painted. While all the houses on the other side of the road were like villas with lawns et al, Green Sanctum Apartments had two floors with a row of maybe three apartments on each floor.

The neighbourhood indicated a certain degree of affluence. They had also caught a hip shopping complex nearby and a few catchy hubs on the way. 'Not bad,' they said in unison with a little giggle to themselves.

With their bags in front of the building, Gopal whipped out his cellphone for a quick selfie. In the distance, he could see three men walking towards them. Two of them, who were further behind the third, were in crisp formal shirts and trousers.

The third man, ahead of the other two, and who was approaching Gopal and Dhara hastily, was in a blue baseball cap, an Aerosmith T-shirt, and denims.

Gopal put his mobile phone aside and looked at this man because it seemed like he wanted to say something. The man came right next to Gopal and Dhara and muttered something under his breath.

Gopal pulled Dhara closer. He was composed but something about this man in casual street-style smarts didn't seem right. Unable to understand what the man was saying, Gopal asked, 'Sorry, are you saying something to me?'

The man now muttered with a little more intent, 'If you are staying with Debbie, tell these people coming behind me that you are her friends who have come over to stay.'

Between a thick Delhi accent and the two thoroughbred Chennai folks, a lot was lost in transit. Gopal repeated, 'Sorry, could you come again?'

'You are here for Debbie, right? Tell these two folks coming behind me that you are her friends. Or just say that you came to meet Debbie at the bar called Cress Bistro. It's around the block in GK-2 Market. Debbie and I will meet you there in fifteen minutes and explain everything.'

Gopal caught the last part fairly well because the man slowed down his speech. He still couldn't understand what the fuss was about. In the interim, the two gentlemen in formals got near Gopal and Dhara.

The taller of the two extended his hand warmly. 'Hi, I am Vikramjeet Saxena. We are with the Delhi Municipal Corporation.' Vikramjeet looked like he made good use of his gym membership.

'This is my colleague Basant Singh,' Vikramjeet said, pointing at the other stocky mustachioed gentleman.

'Hi, I am Gopal.'

Meanwhile, the man in the Aerosmith T-shirt looked askance and went inside the complex of Green Sanctum Apartments.

Dhara's heart rate increased a tad. What could Gopal and Dhara have to do with these folks from the Delhi Municipal Corporation, she wondered.

Vikramjeet continued, 'You are here on vacation, sir, ma'am?'

'That's right, sir,' Gopal deferred.

'Basant and I had a tip-off about an Airbnb renting business here. You see, sir, the city laws do not sanction renting out of rented apartments and we have reason to believe that your owner is doing this illegally.'

Gopal was stumped with this assertion. 'We didn't know about this, sir. We booked our stay on Airbnb's official site. I mean, if we knew . . .'

Dhara jumped in. 'But our host Debbie Malhotra has a listed apartment on the Internet. How can it be allowed on Airbnb if it is illegal?'

'It's not as simple as it looks, ma'am. We suspect that the gentleman in the T-shirt and denims who just went inside is either Debbie's boyfriend or husband. In fact, we have been trying to get a few witnesses for a while, but it looks like we got lucky today,' said Basant. He shrugged his shoulders as he said this.

Dhara and Gopal were flabbergasted.

'But you don't need to worry about anything, ma'am. Your stay won't be affected in any way whatsoever.'

'Okkkayyy . . . So we can go in?' asked Gopal.

'Absolutely. Please feel free to go in. Just one thing . . .' Basant paused. 'As you go inside, we will be taking a few pictures of you walking in. I hope that's no trouble for you,' he added.

'Pictures? Why? We don't want any pictures taken,' Gopal chipped in, feeling a little confident now that this wasn't turning into a mugging incident on the much-disgraced streets of New Delhi.

'Since the original owner passed away, we know Debbie has been doing this illegally over the last few months. We have complaints from her neighbours as well about this.

We need proof for our records and then it's an open-and-shut case,' said Vikramjeet.

Sweet Debbie, thought Dhara, who had promised to take her to the nearby Furniture Market for shopping. Prompt Debbie, thought Dhara, who had replied to every query Gopal and Dhara threw her way. Nice Debbie, who had also thrown in breakfast as part of their stay every day in New Delhi for five days. Who does that! Debbie had only three reviews on the site but all of them were rated five stars. It didn't matter that all the previous guests stayed only one night each. Interacting with Debbie over the last month, Dhara realized why they rated her highly. Because Debbie was exactly how every Airbnb host should be—nice, prompt and sweet.

No, Dhara was not going to let these two Haryanvi inspectors get the better of nice, prompt and sweet Debbie.

'Sorry, we wouldn't like to be photographed. In fact, we wouldn't like to be involved in this altercation between you and Debbie at all,' Dhara spoke up for the first time.

'There is no involvement as such. We will only stand here and take these pictures. That's it. Umm . . . you might need to make an appearance in the court over the next three days. One swift hearing with the judge—two hours is all it will take, I assure you,' pressed Vikramjeet.

Gopal and Dhara exchanged a few short sentences in Tamil.

'Sorry, we are not getting in here,' Dhara said.

'Okay, so where will you go?' an irritated Vikramjeet asked.

'In fact, we are here to go to Cress Bistro, mister. And you are right, we are meeting Debbie there. Do you want to take pictures of us heading towards the bar?' Dhara replied defiantly.

Cress Bistro was a nearby bar in Greater Kailash that came recommended from Debbie during one of the many e-mail exchanges. She said multiple times that Gopal and Dhara must try the food there. It was also rated high on Lonely Planet.

'Listen, ma'am, we can all go back happy if we just nail this Debbie one time. I can't tell you what a witch that woman is. She married her sick landlord just so that she could have this property to herself. That old man, probably thrice her age, kicked the bucket in January. Since then she has been using this property to sublet it on Airbnb,' a serious Vikramjeet ranted.

'You listen, mister. If you have a problem with Debbie, you take it up with Airbnb,' Gopal said.

'Do you know anything about New Delhi's tenancy protection laws, sir?' Basant asked.

'We are done here. Honey, let's head to Cress. It's over the left corner, I think,' said Dhara, turning away from Basant and Vikramjeet and dragging her heavy luggage across the road.

Basant and Vikramjeet, exasperated, could feel the bird getting out of hand. They brought their City Council jeep towards the other end of the road and parked it in front of Green Sanctum Apartments.

Cress Bistro was a dainty little pub laid out with exposed red bricks, a long bar section and plush comfortable leather seats. Gopal, a little distraught with all the mess, managed to get a table with a nice view of Greater Kailash.

'Debbie told me that the chicken here is really good,' said Dhara.

'What are we doing here, Dhara?' asked Gopal.

'What! What do you mean? Debbie told me a lot of affluent people, even actors, frequent this pub because the chicken here is really good,' said Dhara.

'We are on holiday, Dhara. You had no business meddling with those inspectors there. I kept quiet for the most part there because I didn't want to start this holiday with a fight. Why should we care about Debbie? Let's book another room and be done with it.'

'Gopal, we have paid Rs 20,000 for this booking. This was an expensive flat. I don't want to be fighting with Airbnb disputing a claim later. Besides, Debbie and I have exchanged so many messages. I am telling you, she is the sweetest person on earth. Who else has a five-star reviewed apartment in this neighbourhood? Besides, she is also pregnant. Do we want her to be in this mess because of us? Think about it.'

'Dhara, I am not staying in that apartment. There is a nice hotel around the block that we had shortlisted, if you remember. I am going to make a call to get us a booking there for the next five days.'

'Yeah, no problem! But let's just keep that poor woman out of it,' Dhara stated.

Gopal stepped out for ten minutes and came back with a smile on his face. 'That's it. Done. We finish lunch here and take a cab. It's probably a ten-minute drive at best.'

He called for a waiting staff. 'We would like some water.'

Dhara was just reading the menu but thinking about what Debbie might be going through bothered her. 'I hope she is able to sort out her stuff with the officials.'

'I don't know about that. If she is so sweet, why hasn't she called you back till now? That guy said fifteen minutes, right?'

Right about then, Dhara's phone buzzed.

'There you go. She is calling now. Happy?' Dhara jibed.

'Hey Debbie! It's so nice to hear from you. Are you okay?' Dhara answered.

In a quick chat Debbie mentioned that she was speaking from the apartment and could see the inspectors from her window. She apologized multiple times. 'You know these city council inspectors have been trying to malign my name ever since my husband passed away. I know you had to go through a messy start but trust me I have alerted Airbnb about this. Whatever they are saying about sub-letting not being allowed is just not true. There are a million apartments from New Delhi on Airbnb. Where are you guys now?'

'That's all right, Debbie. Both Gopal and I are with you on this. You know it might seem like we have been mailing each other since the last month but it feels like I know you. They wanted to take pictures of us entering the building, but I refused and came straight to Cress Bistro,' said Dhara.

'One chicken tacos, please,' an indifferent Gopal said to the waiting staff. 'And she will tell you what she would like after this call.'

'Dhara, I would have come to meet you at Cress but you know about my pregnancy. I can't move around much. I had a feeling these guys would be there to harass you, which is why I sent over my boyfriend, Pervez, to meet you before you entered.'

She paused for a sigh. Talking so much under stress can't be good for a woman who was expecting, Dhara thought to herself.

Debbie continued. 'Some cranky neighbours who have got poor reviews have also turned against me. I guess both these inspectors got to you before Pervez could explain the situation. Normally, we just say we have friends staying over and it's all fine,' she assured.

Dhara listened to Debbie's concerns with a keen ear.

'I will be sending Pervez over shortly to Cress. You guys just stay there,' Debbie concluded.

'Pervez, her boyfriend, is coming here to meet us,' Dhara brought Gopal up to speed.

She cajoled her husband into meeting Pervez one time before leaving. 'Let's hear their side of the story is all I am saying,' she urged.

'Fine,' Gopal said, expressionless.

Pervez, the man with the Aerosmith T-shirt and faded denims made an entry into Cress ten minutes later. He wasn't wearing the cap any more.

After a calm round of introductions, Pervez explained.

'We are terribly sorry for what happened. The thing is that Debbie was staying with her landlord, Akash Malhotra, in this very building a few years ago. Akash was seventy-one then and didn't have any heir. He fell in love with Debbie and promised her the house, but he passed away before putting it all on paper. Delhi State rules that if one dies without an heir, the apartment is to be transferred to the city council. That's why the city council folks are keeping a watch on this. Debbie, on the other hand, is trying her best to prove how Akash was going to transfer the property to her. Debbie had a few papers ready with her, but the old man passed away a day before he was to sign the will. I am her lawyer who was helping her through the mess of last year and we started spending more time with each other. And . . .'

Pervez stopped. 'We also decided to raise Akash's child together. The child she is pregnant with is Akash's,' he explained.

'That's Akash's child?' Gopal asked, a bit surprised.

'Yeah. I love Debbie so much; it didn't matter to me. Akash was a nice guy. Everyone in the neighbourhood liked him. If only he were around. Pity he didn't live long enough. The irony is that the city inspectors think that this child is mine,' a fretful Pervez added.

'I get it now,' Gopal said. 'But we don't want to be involved in your apartment any more. I mean we should meet socially because my wife would love to meet Debbie, but we are going to write to Airbnb for a full refund as an exception.'

'I know how Debbie and Dhara got along like a house on fire, and we completely understand and appreciate your honesty.' Pervez looked down at the table to gather himself.

'But to be completely honest with you, it just so happens that I was recently fired from my firm and in Debbie's state we could have really done with the money. Could you consider staying over for one night and just pay us Rs 5000? That's all we ask. Besides, even if you file for a refund, it's going to take days and it is always doubtful when and where the money will come from. If you stay over for one night, you can claim a full refund for the remaining Rs 15,000 stating that you didn't like the apartment or that the Wi-Fi wasn't working. I know it's a sticky one but given our situation, it would mean a lot,' pleaded Pervez.

'Allow us some time to discuss this, Pervez,' Gopal requested.

'Of course. Take your time and once again, sorry for the bother,' Pervez said.

He shook Gopal's hand and stood up to leave. Just then Pervez's eyes darted towards the exit and settled on a familiar face. He rushed towards the door.

Debbie, whose picture Dhara could identify from her exchanges on e-mail, was walking into Cress Bistro in an off-white loose dress that was nearly sweeping the floor. Nature had bestowed on Debbie that glow expectant mothers carry. She walked inside slowly even as Pervez reached out to give her a hand. She didn't perhaps need it but lovingly accepted his hand.

Gopal and Dhara both stood up as Pervez and Debbie made their way across to their table.

'I had explicitly told her to not make the effort, but that's Debbie for you. She will do anything for her guests.' Pervez looked at Gopal and Dhara.

Dhara gave Debbie a warm hug.

'Guys, I wanted to reach out personally and thank you for being so kind and patient. But we are all set now,' Debbie reassured them. 'I have spoken to the deputy director of the Municipal Corporation and explained that I listed on Airbnb the day Akash passed away. It keeps a little saving going for the baby and they should consider my case differently. They have agreed to reopen the hearing next month. Everything is sorted now. The good news is you guys are welcome anytime and Pervez can help you with the luggage.'

Gopal and Dhara were relieved to hear this.

'Well, thank you for the offer. And we have heard your side of the story now. Big relief to know that it's all set but we've already looked up another apartment, you know. I mean it's our first trip to New Delhi together and just in case those officials come back again, Dhara and I don't want to be stuck in a courthouse. Or to be honest with you, even indulge in a conversation with them,' Gopal said.

Debbie was a little taken aback with the decision but gathered herself admirably.

'Oh well, okay. If that's your decision it doesn't matter. But, Dhara, tell me where you are staying, all right? I will still take you to the markets we spoke about. It's going to be fun, let me tell you that,' Debbie said with a hint of sadness.

'Absolutely! I have your number and will call you once we settle in. Let's see. Today is Monday, tomorrow we are at Connaught Place. How about Wednesday? I will pack off Gopal to Qutub Minar maybe and I can step out with you?' Dhara said.

'That's perfect! Oh gosh, I think I need to go to the loo,' Debbie excused herself.

Pervez stood up to escort Debbie to the restroom.

'See, I told you, it's all going to be good,' Dhara said.

'Whatever. Not the finest experience, is all,' a grumpy Gopal babbled.

Pervez came back to the table. 'I am glad it all got sorted out. Debbie might want to hang out here for some more time with you guys. I need to leave to deal with some of the legal stuff. Just one last thing, I know you guys have been very patient with us,' he said. 'I feel horrible saying this but Debbie doesn't know about me not having a job, so if you could keep the bit about my offer of one night and the Rs 5000 to yourself . . . I mean if it's not too much to ask.'

'Oh, oh, sure Pervez, no problem,' Gopal said. He was glad that this was all coming to an end.

'Thanks so much, guys! Really appreciate it.'

Suddenly, a loud cry was heard from the restroom. Pervez scurried towards it. He came out in less than thirty seconds without Debbie by his side.

'Her water broke,' Pervez was nervous. 'We have to take her to the hospital. Could you please help and call a cab, Gopal?' Pervez asked. 'I am going to get her out of the restroom,' he said in the same breath.

The other waiting staff too sprang into action. A couple of them ran out with Gopal to flag an auto on the main road.

Pervez, a face of desperation by now, turned towards Dhara. 'This year has been really tough. I am sorry to ask you like this but we were really banking on the Rs 20,000 from you folks. Could you please at least lend me Rs 5000 to take her to the hospital?'

'Of course,' Dhara opened her purse and ruffled through her cash. She handed over ten crisp notes of Rs 500 each. 'You sure this will be enough?' she checked with Pervez.

Pervez had tears in his eyes. No one had ever treated him with such generosity. 'You are a godsend, Dhara. Thank you so very much.' He rushed back towards the restroom and slowly walked out with Debbie completely hanging over him this time, her face red with agony.

Dhara rushed to help. 'Anyone have a wheelchair here? It will really help,' she screamed in perfect Tamilian English in a restaurant full of Delhiites.

In an instant, someone got hold of one and placed it in front of Debbie. She settled in the wheelchair with pain writ all over her being. In the meantime, a cab was ready at the entrance of Cress Bistro.

It took some time for Debbie to settle in completely. She was writhing in pain.

Pervez went over to Dhara and Gopal and held their hands. 'Thank you so much. This will stay with us for a lifetime. If you guys are around, would love for you to come and see our baby. We will be at the Saket Maternity Ward. See you guys, and more importantly, happy holidays!'

'Good luck, Debbie, Pervez,' screamed Dhara. 'It will be fine.'

'Oh, I sure hope so,' Debbie convulsed with pain in the cab.

'Have you thought of enough boy and girl names? This is so exciting.'

'I will message you or call you. I promise,' Debbie's eyes were nearly closing.

The taxi sped off.

'What a town, this Delhi!' sighed Dhara. 'So much drama in so little time.'

'I know!' a relieved Gopal said. 'Time to get back to our tacos.'

They went in, hand in hand, perhaps a little more in love with each other than from an hour before.

A month later, Prof. Albert Costanza at the National School of Drama addressed the 2017 summer graduation batch in a room full of students and acclaimed professors.

'Great performances demand meticulous preparation, which in itself impels a merciless dedication to our craft. And then comes the denouement which, if it is anything less than flawless, could make the whole thing fall apart like a stack of cards. As great a cradle for acting as the hallowed walls of this institution can be, it still requires real men and women to go out there and perform often without gratuity but just so that the human soul is shaken with empathy. And for doing that, the winner of this year's Abraham Alkazi Scholarship for Outstanding Live Experimental Theatre goes to . . .'

A deafening applause filled the National School of Drama auditorium as Vikramjeet, Basant, Pervez and Debbie stood up to head towards the stage.

A week later, Dhara received a deposit of Rs 5000 in her bank account from an unknown sender. 'This must be nice, sweet and prompt Debbie,' she told Gopal. 'I knew she would return the money, even though she never told me what they named their child.'

While this story is fictionalized, it is based on a real-life incident that happened with me and my wife as we were checking into our Airbnb pad on Melrose Avenue in Los Angeles. We had just offloaded our luggage, when the municipal inspectors turned up requesting to take photographs of us entering the apartment so that those could be used against the landlady. She was eight months pregnant at the time.

Airbnb was more than kind to refund the money when we wrote to them about the issue.

Lights, Camera, Cut

'How will I know whom to sell DVDs to?' Budhia, the security guard at the hallowed National School of Drama vented his ire to Mohanty, the tea vendor. Budhia was particularly incensed because of the newly received missive from Prof. Albert Costanza of the Alternative Films and Theatre Division fame.

He continued, 'The normal scrap-metal guys here have no use for DVDs. And this professor has been after my life to create space for new journals in the library.'

Mohanty, who was more interested in selling an extra cup of tea, pretended to empathize with a couple of nods. 'Should I fill one more cup? This time with extra cardamom,' he egged Budhia.

'No, bhai. One cup during the day only. Anyway, you please ask around if any of your guys can take some 500 DVDs from here. The professor will practically give them away for free.'

'What does one do with these DVDs?' Mohanty asked.

'These are films, very good films, but not like the ones that you and I watch. These are international films. Old but very good. One can rent them and make some extra money on the side. Will help if you know your films,' Budhia said, savouring the last gulp from his glass. Mohanty's tea was a stellar brew.

Mohanty bid goodbye to Budhia and went on his way towards the next road where his patrons from various government offices descended at 11 a.m. every day for mid-morning tea. This is where he made most of his money. The visit to Budhia was purely a ceremonial start to his day. There were no more than a handful of customers at the National School of Drama, but he liked talking to the whiny Budhia. There was always something wrong with his life that Budhia couldn't wait to talk about.

That June 2008 night, while Mohanty counted his savings for the year, he thought it was time to invest in a new business. The conversation around DVDs and starting a rental shop wasn't a bad one, he deduced. For months now, Mohanty's friend Jagannath had been persuading him to start a cigarette stall near Regal in Connaught Place.

'Customers keep floating all through the day. Not like your tea business, where you must drag your cycle along,' Jagannath reasoned with Mohanty.

Since he was familiar with Regal, Mohanty knew many people who would come and watch English films in Connaught Place. The thought that he could rent a corner shop near Regal and run his tea business alongside was worth considering. Besides, his fifteen-year-old Atlas cycle was getting creakier by the day and Jagannath had promised to find a corner shop for under Rs 15,000 per month.

'Imagine how much time you will save if you don't have to travel from office to office,' Jagannath said.

'But right now, I don't have any rent expense, Jaggan. If I take the spot, I can't do only the tea business from there. For the new extra rent, I will have to find a new business to add to my tea vending,' Mohanty declared.

The next morning, he went to see Jagannath in Connaught Place with the proposition of starting a DVD-renting business. 'Sounds like a great idea. I know how many DVDs sell in Palika Bazaar every month. It's a superb business. Don't lose a moment on this and get them all.'

That's all the encouragement Mohanty needed to land up at the National School of Drama the next morning to see his friend Budhia.

'Hand me the DVDs. I will take them,' Mohanty said to a perplexed Budhia.

Budhia was happy that his problem of clearing the DVDs was out of his way. He had been asking people around for over a week and Mohanty was the only one who had come back to take away the DVDs.

Budhia led him from the entrance of the imposing building towards a third-floor room that was uncomfortably muggy. Like an old library, long rows of bookshelves ran from one end of the room to the other. Columns of dusty DVDs that looked like they hadn't been touched in ages stood in wait for a redeemer and here was Mohanty.

Budhia took Mohanty through the various sections that were segregated per language. English, French, Hindi, Bengali. Overall, Budhia pegged the number at 474 DVDs. Mohanty ran his fingers against some of those and tried recollecting some of those films. But except a handful of Amitabh Bachchan titles, Mohanty recognized none of the others.

'Are these any good? I see no Dharmendra or Vinod Khanna in here,' he was reconsidering his decision now.

'What the hell you talking about? People would kill for this collection. Look at this,' Budhia pulled out a tape from the French section. 'This is Godard's entire collection and this is *Breathless*, his most famous film. Your customers would go crazy. What more can you ask for?'

Mohanty had never heard the name Godard before.

'If these are so good, why do you need to get rid of them?'

'I told you, the new professor wants to bring some new journals. He is also getting some new format called Blu-Ray for these films. Better looking for students, he says.'

'How much do you want for the whole thing?'

'I don't know. Whatever you think is the right price.'

Jagannath had told Mohanty not to give anything more than thousand rupees for the collection.

'Five hundred rupees. That's it. I don't have more than that and I will have to do two rounds in an auto. That's extra expense for me. Besides, my friend tells me it will be expensive to find a place to sell these DVDs,' Mohanty meandered.

'All yours!' Budhia gleamed with a victorious smile.

Mohanty dragged the DVDs in six different gunny sacks to his modest dwelling near Mandi House. He laid these on his bed and on the floor and arranged the titles in alphabetical order. Next, he and Jagannath found a place for displaying these titles right next to Regal.

At a rent of Rs 15,000, and well within a week of his first conversation with Budhia about the DVD's, Mohanty was all set with his DVD store, which he named 'Stories', with a large poster of Jean-Luc Godard on the adjoining pillar. It was a throwaway handed by Budhia from the archives. 'This poster *toh* people will go mad for, take it from me,' said a boastful Budhia.

The first morning, as he was setting up the DVDs with this poster outside his makeshift shop, a granny walking with her twin granchildren waved out to him. He waved back. He couldn't hear what she was saying from the other end of the road so one of the twins crossed the road to speak to Mohanty.

'Nana is asking if you have a Godard film called *Breathless*,' the child asked.

Without blinking an eyelid, Mohanty replied, 'I most definitely do.'

Over the next month, with a little word here and there, and especially with the walk-in crowd around Regal, Mohanty rented out over 300 films. Every morning between 10–11 a.m., old people from the neighbourhood thronged outside his shop and discussed films to rent out from Stories. He charged a full Rs 100 for each DVD. He thought he could always reduce the price if customers didn't buy, but this was Central Delhi. Customers came in droves.

The next month the local edition of *Mid-Day* listed his store as a DVD library for great old classics. Suddenly, Stories became the cynosure of Connaught Place. Mohanty hired an assistant to keep track of all the deliveries. While his old Atlas cycle still came in handy, he bought a new one for his assistant.

One of his customers, a Mrs Roy, whose teenage grandchild Akash loved all sorts of obscure films, offered to find him a slightly bigger place as the pedestrian traffic wasn't conducive to good discussions around films. In exchange, Akash asked that Mrs Roy be allowed to borrow any DVD anytime for free. Mohanty agreed. He began to spend more time now in his newly instituted DVD business than tea-making. A month later, a new store was inaugurated across the road from Regal with an even bigger signage of Stories.

Mohanty bought a DVD player for himself and started enjoying some of the recommended classics by his customers. Films by renowned film-makers both from India and abroad, Sai Paranjpe, Ritwik Ghatak, Satyajit Ray, Bimal Roy, John Ford, Alfred Hitchcock were raging hits among his customers. Next, he wanted to understand Hollywood films better, so Mohanty started English lessons with a nearby coaching institute in the evenings.

It helped that all the English DVDs came with subtitles. In less than three months, he had exhausted all the English films from his collection. Thereafter, he started with the French films of the masters from the 1950s and 1960s. Melville, Godard, Truffaut, he saw them all. More importantly, he spent time understanding the various techniques of cinema by investing in books around film-making.

In less than a year since having bought the archival collection from the National School of Drama, Mohanty had a thriving business. Soon DVD agents of production houses like Sony and Reliance got in touch with Mohanty and requested them to carry their new Hindi films. Mohanty expanded his DVD library over the next few years and started carrying all the latest films now. It wasn't just about old classics any more.

Mohanty bought a mobile phone for the first time in his life in 2009 and realized the benefits that technology had bestowed on the modern man. Confident of the business, Mohanty committed to a ten-year lock-in lease for the store with a minimum guaranteed rent for the landlord till 2020.

By now, Mohanty was well-versed with the language of cinema. Whether it was talking about the different eras, genres or auteurs of world cinema—Mohanty could outwit anyone in a conversation about films. Spending time at the store meant that Mohanty would often watch two to three films a day. And then came the more interesting part of talking about these films with his customers, which he enjoyed thoroughly.

The more films Mohanty watched, the more he cared to read about them. He developed a keen eye for the craft of cinema. He considered the French thrillers of the '50s and the '60s the Bible among all things cinema, and a certain Jean-Luc Godard became his much-revered idol. He had seen *Breathless* countless times and the likes of *Alphaville, Pierret Le Fou* and *Vivre Sa Vie* were his staple films to fall back on whenever a day proved too cumbersome.

He even thought about renting a crew and shooting a film based on a script he would write himself, but Jagannath thankfully talked him out of it. He challenged Jagannath by saying, 'Maybe a film is what we can leave this world with our names on it. Let's think of something to make.' But gradually Jagannath's sane arguments won Mohanty over.

However, that didn't stop Mohanty from reading and watching more cinema. In and around Connaught Place, he would be invited for local film premieres by people who were at the fringes of the entertainment industry. With his measured manner of speaking and his newly gained knowledge of films, Mohanty charmed whoever he met. There was always that element of surprise about how a simpleton like Mohanty could talk about French crime thrillers and German Noir with elan. He would always leave a note with the people he met from the industry that if they ever were thinking of shooting a film, he would be glad to help them.

The time to make a film, however, was running out as the years went by like a breeze. He spent most of his twenties taking care of his parents. His thirties went by in selling tea. In his forties, he was busy building Stories. The times when he missed female companionship, on weekends, he kept himself occupied by attending screenings or reading about films.

He got himself a second-hand laptop that he used to watch YouTube interviews with famous directors, writers, cinematographers and editors by the dozen. That he wasn't hitched so far was not exactly a hitch for him. He had his films and Godard to thank.

In 2015, for the first time, revenues from Stories showed a decline. The younger demographic in Delhi had moved towards illegal online downloads and the raging hot trend of video streaming. All the new films would also come on television within a month and there was no shortage of new English and foreign movie channels.

Mohanty believed great cinema needed to be distributed as freely and frequently as possible otherwise art might not grow to be as eternal as it should be. Such liberal thinking wasn't good for business, Jagannath warned him.

Mohanty's life had changed for the better thanks to his love for cinema. A tea vendor had even become a prime minister in this country, and there he was, another tea vendor who was now invited for some of the biggest film parties in New Delhi. 'I'll be fine. People who love cinema will keep coming to my store, and people who love cinema only grow year after year,' Mohanty would tell Jagannath.

While a few small online rental players like SeventyMM were already available in the country by then, 2016 proved to be a watershed year with a string of high-profile video streaming platform launches that included biggies like Flixtser and Star Videos. That year, except for the holiday season of November, each month registered a decline in visitors to the store as more and more people started discovering their favourite films on these streaming sites.

In December 2016, a panic-stricken Mohanty revamped his store and gave it a new look. For the inventory that seldom moved from his store, he announced a throwaway sale. The number of customers he got that day was a glimmer of hope that Stories might just weather the storm. In addition, he halved his store space to reduce his rent.

He also let go off his trusted assistant and started negotiations with his landlord, the forever grumpy Ranjit Khanna, to reduce the lock-in period to eight years instead of ten.

'What if you can't pay for next year again?' growled Ranjit.

'I intend to take a salaried job. I have sent out feelers to my customers already. I will meet the rent commitment for 2017,' assured Mohanty.

On 1 March 2017, Mohanty put a telltale signage on his beloved store that had served him well for so many years.

'CLOSING DOWN SALE' it read. 'ALL STOCK MUST GO,' the signage pleaded.

Loyal customers of Stories came from all over the city to offer their commiserations. It was the fraternity of film lovers with exquisite taste. They knew their Ritwik from their Satyajit and their Ford from their Scorsese. That March, every evening was like a little party in the Outer Circle lane outside Mohanty's store.

While they all had come to buy the DVDs that were available at the closing down sale, the truth was that they were crying inside. Oh, for how many evenings had this little store taken away their misery because Mohanty recommended the right film for their mood. And now all of them must depend on some faceless, heartless, computer-generated algorithm for a choice of a film for the evening. How low had civilization stooped, they pondered. And then they all went away for new year shopping with their families, while Mohanty desolately walked to his house in Mandi House.

The only DVDs that Mohanty kept for himself were a few of his Godard favourites. He remembered how this was the first film that was rented from his store.

The lone bright spot that dark month was that Mohanty got a new job. He was relieved that his new job still had something to do with his beloved cinema. Mrs Roy's son was now a sales manager at PVR Cinemas and he offered Mohanty a job as an usher.

Mohanty was filled with gratitude towards Akash. Pity was, unlike before, he couldn't repay him in any manner. The other option, which was perhaps a more stable job, was offered by one of Jagannath's friends. It was to man the Delhi Metro rail platforms as a security guard with flexible hours. Mohanty preferred to be an usher simply because Akash had thrown in a trump card that allowed Mohanty to watch any film during off-peak hours without buying a ticket.

Thus, on 2 April 2017, Mohanty Sarkar began a new life at the age of sixty-two at PVR Cinemas in Connaught Place. He smiled warmly at all the ticket holders and looked at their seat numbers on the tickets before guiding them to their seats. Some smiled back and some scoffed but no one ever spoke. If only someone would talk to him about the climax. Or about the first act setup. But no. It was all about 'Three rows up, ma'am, first seat to the left' or some such one-sided tepid verbal snack.

Over the next month though, Mohanty made peace with his new job. But his overall cinema consumption came down considerably. He didn't have the same drive to talk about cinema either. Occasionally, he would speak with Akash about any upcoming French film and that was that.

One night in October, as Mohanty saw everyone out from the last show that ended at 11.30 p.m., he observed an infirm old man who was attended by another man alongside him, trying to walk towards the exit slowly. Mohanty didn't remember ushering this old gentleman in. Maybe he had got in from the other entrance, where his colleague Kumar was stationed, Mohanty reasoned. Kumar was nowhere to be seen now, so Mohanty patiently waited for the two men to come out.

As they approached the exit, Mohanty caught a closer look at the old man. He seemed familiar. His spectacles were particularly reminiscent of someone he knew. And then it struck him.

'Mr Godard!' Mohanty choked.

'May I,' he offered his hand to the great auteur.

A younger gentleman in a black suit, next to Godard, politely interrupted in a French accent, 'He is fine. Thank you for asking. He is actually . . .'

But Mohanty Sarkar was seeing stars. He didn't hear a word of what the man in the black suit said. Now breathing heavily, Mohanty said, 'It has been my lifelong dream to meet you, sir! I have seen all your films. Even the ones from way back in the '60s. They were the very *raison d'être* of my existence not too long ago, sir,' Mohanty said, feeling rather smug about throwing in that timely French phrase.

Mr Godard, frail of age and heavy of breath, couldn't comprehend this fast-paced slur of words coming in from Mohanty. He questioningly looked at the younger man in the black suit and slowly uttered, 'Remi . . .'

Remi went on to translate for Godard what Mohanty said. Mohanty regained his breath and continued.

'Please tell him. I have seen them all. *Les Carabiniers, Le Gai Savour, Tout Va Bien,*' Mohanty started reeling the names of them all, in French. He deliberately didn't mention *Breathless*. Everyone who knows anything about Godard would talk about *Breathless*, but Mohanty was the true connoisseur. He had seen the lesser known ones, the failed ones and the ones that by every measure were better than *Breathless*.

Something caught Godard's attention and he mumbled something in French to Remi. Remi clarified, 'Mr Godard wants to know where you saw *Les Carabiniers*.'

'I had a DVD store that I ran till last year. The first DVD I rented out was yours, sir. And it had a big poster of yours in front of it. It was the riot, sir. I had to shut down the store because the video streaming trend killed my business.'

Godard sighed and gave a disappointed look.

And then Godard spoke in a measured voice to Remi. From his tone, Mohanty sensed this was important. Remi patiently let Godard finish his sentence.

After what seemed like an eternity once Godard stopped speaking, Remi said, 'Mr Godard is sad to hear about your store shutting down. He has been looking for a copy of *Les Carabiniers* for a long time. They had given the film to a film-restoration company but while restoring it to DVD, they missed a few frames that were very dear to him. He wished your store hadn't closed down, otherwise he would've liked to visit you to see the DVD of *Les Carabiniers*. It's a film that he holds very close to his heart. Thank you for your kindness though. We must be on our way now.'

Mohanty's heart leapt a thousand times while he heard this from Remi. 'No, no, no. I still do have the DVD of the film. Please tell him I have kept a few copies of my favourite Godard films. And I will be able to give him a copy if he so wishes.'

Remi relayed the information to Godard, at which point the old man had a sudden burst of energy to his voice. He spoke to Mohanty in poetic French, looking at his eyes with much kindness and love. Remi spoke an instant later. 'Mr Godard will be very grateful to you if this could be arranged. He thanks the Good Lord that he met you today. It is actually Mr Godard's final wish that he wants to see this particular film with his grandchildren before he dies.'

Mohanty suddenly realized the significance of the last statement. As a third-generation tea vendor, Mohanty's life fortunes had got him to the point where he could lend a helping hand in fulfilling a wish of the greatest director in the world.

He collected himself and said, 'Well, you have no clue how lucky I am to be hearing from Mr Godard and seeing him in person. Could you tell me where you are staying? I shall head home right away and bring it to the hotel.'

'We are at the Le Meridien. We leave early morning so we don't wish to bother you, but tonight is the only night we have.'

'I understand. That won't be a problem at all. I should be able to drop it at the hotel by midnight. Shall I leave it in your name?'

'Yes, that would be perfect.'

Godard had a beatific smile on his face by now and extended his hand warmly to Mohanty. Mohanty, moved by the gesture, kept a real brave face to not well up with a tear. It felt like he was shaking hands with a celestial power. He felt a warm rush of blood through his veins as his hand clasped Godard's.

His final words to Mohanty were in pure Victorian English, 'Thank you and good night.'

Mohanty saw Godard slowly walk back with Remi.

That night, Mohanty went back to his home in Mandi House and turned it upside down. He remembered distinctly that he had *Les Carabiniers* among the eight films of Godard he had kept for himself when he shut down the store for the last time. These were the only films he wanted to retain for himself.

Mohanty checked under the mattress, in his trunk, repeatedly swept the floor under the bed and went through all the smelly leather bags he had, which contained old records of his customers from the store. He had them all except those of the clearance sale. Did someone flick that DVD from under his nose? Or did he end up mixing the DVDs with someone else? It was impossible to track who might have taken that DVD now.

He sat in the middle of his room and contemplated a thousand ways in which he could source *Les Carabiniers* this night for Godard. There was no way out. He was crestfallen.

As the night wore on, Mohanty felt worse about letting down the great Jean-Luc Godard of all people. Imagine, the one person who had such an influence on his life over the last ten years, and whose films he revered like a disciple, was waiting in a room in central Delhi upon Mohanty's given word.

Mohanty's whole life flashed before his eyes. By all accounts, it was a decent life but maybe he had outlived his time. Could he wake up the next morning, thinking that he had nothing to show for ten years in the profession of admiring the magic of films? Tonight's failure was an indisputable sign that this life was not worth living any more.

An inconsolable Mohanty went back to the metro station and threw himself under the last train to Dwarka.

Meanwhile, back at the Le Meridien, Godard, old as he was, spoke cheerily with Remi in French as they dressed for the night, like only father and son can.

Remi was clenching his stomach in a sudden fit of laughter, 'These Indians, such naïve hero-worshippers. They will believe anything. But, father, haven't I told you before that you look like Godard?'

'Yes, you have,' said the father, Pierre Lacour.

'This guy was the absolute pits. How idiotic can the fanatics of filmdom be?'

'Don't delay the gag, though. Once he comes to the hotel, buy him a warm drink and maybe even get him a room here. He deserves a good night's sleep,' said Pierre before slipping himself underneath the comfortable satin sheets.

Most of my education around film classics and world cinema is thanks to a store called Habitat Music and Movies on Church Street in Bengaluru. It housed an enviable collection of DVDs that had some unique labelling such as 'Limelight' and 'Limelight Plus' and 'On Request'. The last was seldom on display and made available only for customers who requested the specific title. Back then in 2008, I would rent a film a day from the store. I left the city in 2009 and returned in 2012. By then, Habitat had shut down. My current DVD dig is 'Once More Video' in Indiranagar, whose owner tells me, 'Not only do they not make movies like they did before, they don't even rent DVDs like they used to.'

I would be surprised if the store is still around by the time this book releases. But if it is, do look it up. You will find a genial man, only too happy to help you with a recommendation.

Run, Zelda, Run

Every year hundreds of runners descend in New Delhi from around the world to participate in the New Delhi Half Marathon. Scores of such visitors stay at the Le Meridien near Connaught Place. Some would be serious runners trying to better their time, while others hoped to check a box of having finished a half marathon.

Ravin Chatterjee had been with the Le Meridien for close to a decade, ever since he joined work after completing his master's in hotel management from IHM, New Delhi. So much had changed in these ten years. In these years, Ravin went from having a thick mop of hair to what could now be described as a steadily receding hairline. His friends from that batch who had joined the Le Meridien had all moved on, but every year he saw those familiar faces that came to the hotel during the week leading up to the half marathon.

There was that elegant oriental lady who never spoke a word and simply handed over her passport. She had affectionate eyes and salt-and-pepper hair. Her lithe body spoke volumes about what a fantastic runner she might have been. Then there was a French father-son duo. The father, who bore an uncanny resemblance to French film-maker Godard, was perhaps in New Delhi every year only to accompany his son who looked like the runner of the two. These were the ones Ravin was accustomed to seeing since

2007. Acknowledging them with a warm twinkling smile only added to the charm of working in a world-class hotel like the Le Meridien.

And then there were the new ones who came every single year, with whom one ends up having benign small talk, like Ravin did with that leggy blonde who sauntered in with the air of a princess.

'Are you here for the half marathon?' Ravin prodded, tucking his belly in at the same time in an attempt to appear fitter than he was.

'Indeed, I am,' Zelda replied with a Russian accent, handing over her passport. Her immaculate hair and her thick eyelashes were thorough distractions, but Ravin was an equally thorough professional.

'Good luck for the run,' he said and simultaneously sighed from within. Her face had a glow that was unreal. Involuntarily, when he stole a glance at her body, he wondered if she was a ballerina.

It was just another day in the office for Ravin. Pretty women walked into his hotel all the time, but Zelda had something about her that made him want to continue the conversation. Except that the check-in was all done and Zelda was set to head to her room.

She shot back a question at Ravin as she collected her passport, 'Are you running too?'

'Yeah, I am.' It was the most ordinary question, and yet Ravin felt like he was getting hot under his collar. He didn't want to continue this conversation.

'What are you shooting for?'

Runners and their timings were inseparable but Ravin had only registered because there was a special price for

Le Meridien employees to register for the run and the entire staff had signed up. Most of them had even set a target time for themselves. His boss, Kunal Tarapore, was going for an hour and forty-five minutes. 'My aim is the Boston Marathon in 2020,' he had told Ravin.

Ravin didn't understand the fascination serious runners had to improve their timings, but he knew that running a half-marathon under two hours was an incredible feat for amateur runners. Though that would be a real stretch for a non-serious runner like Ravin, he didn't want to come across as a complete novice in front of Zelda. He went with a safe estimate.

'Two hours and thirty minutes, I guess,' he mumbled.

Zelda was surprised. Ravin was a lean, well-built man. Most men she knew back in Russia of Ravin's frame comfortably finished a half-marathon in under two hours.

'You can do better than that,' she told Ravin. 'In fact, I could see you doing it in under two hours with three months of training.' The way she said it reflected a certain interest that she perhaps didn't express with everyone, but Ravin chose to ignore it.

'I am a newbie runner. I am going with low benchmarks.'

'Your low benchmark should be 2.15. Not a minute more. Trust me.'

'How can you be so confident?'

'I am a certified RunTracker coach. I train amateur athletes back in Moscow.'

Ravin felt the degrees of separation between him and Zelda diminish. RunTracker, that popular GPS-enabled running app that runners around the world used to train, was nestled in Ravin's phone too.

'Wow. That's amazing. I use RunTracker too. But I guess that's where the similarity ends. What are you gunning for?'

'An hour and twenty. Or thereabouts.'

Ravin was stunned. By every measure, Zelda, for someone in her early thirties as attested by her passport, was a fit woman. She stood tall and straight and her lean arms and legs indicated a certain competency but an hour and twenty was a ridiculous time to finish a half marathon.

'I don't know what to say. You are going to win this whole damn thing, aren't you?'

She laughed with a rhythm that swept Ravin off the carpet he was on.

'No, silly. The winner is probably doing an hour and ten minutes or less. I haven't even checked what the records are.' With that accent, she didn't even sound arrogant.

'You are a modest woman, ma'am. That's what I have learned tonight. Anyway, you are all set. Here's your passport.'

'Thank you, Ravin. It was nice chatting with you. Good luck with your run too. Honestly, timing doesn't matter. I have run long enough in my life to tell you this.'

'Oh, come on. Everyone runs for a better time. I wish I had a coach like you. I could've done something for a better time.'

A voice buzzed inside Ravin's head: *Stop it right there. This woman is a guest at the hotel.*

'You know what. We still have a week. How about you let me train you for the next five days? You rest on Saturday and go for the big run on Sunday.'

Ravin was a bit embarrassed that a hotel guest of all people should offer to help better his running time. But he thought of this as a good break. He could surely do with some help. If that help came in the form of someone as divine as Zelda, it couldn't hurt.

But he couldn't ask for help. Well-intentioned as Zelda's plan might have been, Ravin had to maintain a level of distance from his guests. He had done that for ten years now. No matter how attractive the proposition of spending time with Zelda was, he was determined to resist the temptation.

'I would've loved to, ma'am, but we keep such odd hours at the hotel,' he declined with a smile on his face and a pinch in his heart.

Zelda, on the other hand, didn't even pretend as if she heard him.

'Come on, show me how you fared on your past runs,' she extended her hand for his phone.

As luck would have it, the lobby was deserted and there was no one else around.

Without saying a word, Ravin took out his mobile phone, turned on the RunTracker app and handed it over to Zelda.

Zelda smiled as she went through his timings. 'You mind if I keep this for the next couple of hours? I am going to look at your running patterns and then draw up a plan for the next five days.'

It wasn't leaving the mobile phone with her that bothered him. 'Well, I don't know how to say this. But you are a professional coach. I don't feel comfortable availing your services without a fee.'

'Don't worry about it. It's just five days. It's nothing,' saying so Zelda smiled and turned back to head to her hotel room.

As she walked away, Ravin wondered if he had done the right thing, but his mind was racing with the list of possibilities the next five days might entail.

Later that night, she sent his phone back through a concierge. She also left a message for him on RunTracker. *'Good night, Ravin. Will send you your plan tomorrow.'*

'Thanks, Zelda. You are an angel to do this,' he replied.

'I don't do it for everyone. There's something about you that I think I can work with,' she wrote back. And followed it up with a ;-).

Ravin thought of Zelda all night long. For the short time he managed to grab a nap, he dreamt of her. That's the problem when you are single, he surmised. Every half-decent conversation with a lady seems to throw open a world of fantasies. But Zelda was a tourist. There's no good that can come off any attachment with a foreigner, he concluded.

He shut his eyes and mentally took stock of the stationary needs in the hotel to take his mind off her. It was of little help.

Zelda had asked him to be ready by 6 a.m. It was a foggy November morning, and like an eager school kid awaiting his favourite teacher, Ravin was ready with his best running apparel and gear at the assigned spot near the exit gate of the hotel. He waited for ten minutes and wasn't sure if he should call her that early in the morning. He looked at the time once again on his mobile phone. That's when he noticed a notification on the RunTracker app. He opened it and saw a message from Zelda.

'Here's your training plan for today,' it said. Alongside the message there were a series of instructions of warm-up exercises to be done, the sprint plan to be followed and video links about the exact posture to be maintained while performing those exercises. He noticed she had added him as a friend on the app. Right then, he received a message from her, 'Have you started?'

Ravin had assumed that Zelda would be there in person to help him train, but clearly she had her methods cut out. It was professional and outright serious. He typed *'Yes'* in reply to her message and then he texted her. *'Are you running as well?'*

Pat came a reply. 'I just got done. I was up at 4.30 a.m.'

It was such an impassionate reply that Ravin thought it best to get on with his training for the day. Over the next few days, the routine repeated itself. Zelda sent Ravin his set of exercises and running plan for each of the next four days. Ravin exhausted himself following the suggested plan. On the third day, he was barely able to cope up with the sprint plan. But he did it thinking of Zelda. Strangely, it meant something to Ravin to please her.

He sent a report back to Zelda after his workout every single day. And every time he messaged her, he received a short *'Good!'* or *'Well done!'* in reply. Apart from the two specific communication windows before and after his workout, Zelda never texted Ravin.

Ravin had the option to find her number from the hotel system and text her but that would've been an invasion of guest privacy. So, he texted her on RunTracker:

'How are your preparations coming along?'

He once again received a terse *'Good!'* as a reply.

Perhaps she was a woman of few words. Ravin was curious about Zelda's whereabouts during the day but like a good student he thought it best to finish his plan before asking her. A day later, the desire to call her on her mobile phone reared its head. Once again, Ravin muffled it. It was not as if he was looking to date her, but maybe a single meeting before she left on Sunday evening would be good, he thought.

'Closure is important in life. In relationships and at work,' the disciplined Kunal Tarapore's wisdom rang in his ears. It's something Kunal said often while giving advice to young management trainees on how to deal with external vendors.

Ravin felt great on Friday evening. He had done every single exercise in the exact intended manner that Zelda sent his way over the past few days. While Zelda's plan didn't include any long-distance run in these five days, Ravin felt good about the Sunday run. It was perhaps also a good time to thank Zelda for the time she had put in.

But he had no way to reach out to Zelda. Besides, Indian men could come across as stalkers and Ravin didn't want to join that dubious club by looking up her number from the customer database. He was doing well so far, he told himself.

He concluded that Friday would be a good day to ask her if she was free for the evening. He could buy Zelda a nice dinner to thank her for her intervention. Finally, after waiting all day, hoping she would send him a message, he turned to RunTracker to pop the question.

'Hey Zelda, are you around? I was wondering if you're free for dinner or a coffee. It would be great to thank you in person for the training. I have never felt better than in this one week.'

He didn't hear back from her. That night he tossed and turned in his bed a million times and checked his phone another million times. He couldn't sleep. It wasn't the best lead-up to his run. He shouldn't have got carried away. This had to be kept extremely professional from the very start. But, by now, his colleagues had seen him put in the effort the past five days. No one knew it was Zelda for whom Ravin had been putting in those hours.

'You seem to be gunning for the Boston Marathon next year itself,' Kunal had joked with him on Friday.

It was a comment that he waved off nonchalantly. His only motivation now was to run the damn thing and be done with it once and for all. After this, he was going to get back to being Ravin Chatterjee, the upright and professional duty manager of the Le Meridien, New Delhi. He cursed himself for not being able to get Zelda out of his mind.

The next morning, a bleary-eyed Ravin reached out for his phone on the side of his bed. There was a new notification from RunTracker. The notification popped: *You have one unread message from Zelda.*

'Finally,' he mumbled and straightened himself to read the message. She might have been busy with her preparations of her run; he gave her the benefit of doubt and excitedly went to the Unread Messages section on the app.

The message from Zelda read: '*Congratulations, you have finished Zelda Boskovic's free elite trial plan. To upgrade, click here and see fantastic results with your running. Special offer price only Rs 12,000 for 3 months!*'

The last line stung him the most. It read, '*Exclusively personalized for Ravin Chatterjee by Zelda Boskovic.*'

He knew it was anything but.

Beyond Words

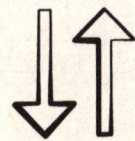

One evening, spent ruminating over Old Monk about what he should do for his career, Pervez Dastur came across an advertisement for an International Film Festival at the India Habitat Centre in New Delhi.

Little did he know that spending those five days shuttling between different auditoriums and listening to eminent writers like Terry Rossio, Bob Peterson and John August would have such an impact on his life that he would apply for the Writing Programme at the Film and Television Institute of India (FTII), Pune, in less than a month. He drew on his savings for the past ten years and paid his fees after an intense round of screening that ended with him winning a seat at the holy grail of film-making education in India.

Pervez left his plush hospitality job in Gurgaon and moved to Pune with dreams of making it big in Bollywood someday. Most people thought it was a crazy decision to leave a well-established corporate career and give it all up to gain entry into the notoriously fickle world of film-making, but that's the kind of epoch-making year 2016 was in Pervez's life.

To say that Pervez struggled during his initial days at FTII was an understatement. While coming up with topics for potential screenplays during workshops, he could never think on the lines of the more adventurous genres of science fiction or fantasy or animation. His story suggestions were pretty run-of-the-mill that never enthused any instructor in his writing workshops.

Upon seeing Pervez struggle, his favourite instructor, Shekhar Apte, a middle-aged scraggy-haired film guru, met him over coffee.

'I can't think of any out-of-the-world experience to put in my writing, like you keep saying. When the other instructors ask me to think out of the box, all I can think of are stories around Gurgaon,' Pervez explained his dilemma to Shekhar.

Shekhar had been an instructor at FTII for eight years and by now had seen every kind of student and tackled every kind of question that a student in distress could come up with.

'Why do you want to be a writer?' Shekhar asked.

'To create something that lives after me.'

Shekhar mulled over this statement. It seemed genuine. The best students always gave a genuine answer. After a couple of minutes of silence, he said, 'Do you know what makes great stories?'

It was too open-ended a question for Pervez. Lots of things made for great stories, the plot points, the characters, the surprise twists, the works. He didn't know what to begin with. Hesitantly, Pervez replied, 'Great characters?'

'I know you are going to list a bunch of things, but here's what I think makes for great stories.'

'What?'

'Your experiences.'

'I have had my share of experiences,' Pervez said.

'Everyone has. But what's unique about yours? Do you have an experience that's so different that you can put it in your writing? About how that experience moved you or devastated you? It could be the love for a woman that you could wage a war for, or even a pain in your heart that is so searing that you wished you weren't breathing?'

Pervez tried to process everything Shekhar said. He had nothing to say in reply.

He had grown up in a protected family of an educated middle-class household in the heartland of affluent north India. He had everything he needed in his childhood. Did he ever have to struggle for anything? Perhaps not, up until this point when he was struggling to come up with new ideas for stories. Neither had he ever experienced any loss of love that he couldn't gather himself back from. Pervez merely gazed at the table mat in front of him.

Shekhar continued. 'Some students have a tireless imagination and they leverage that to conjure up worlds of fantasy. The others rely deeply on their experiences to make them better writers. You must find those experiences here in Pune if you didn't get them in Gurgaon.'

'Nobody likes stories based in Pune. You don't either,' Pervez said.

'I don't because it's easy. And I would like to push my students into territories that they haven't yet gone into,' explained Shekhar.

Pervez loved Shekhar Apte for this very reason. Shekhar was already working on a couple of writing projects for Disney India. Time was a scarce resource for him. And yet he took out time to sit across the table from a newbie like Pervez and advise him. Shekhar did it of his own volition because that's how much educating his students about the craft of screenwriting meant to him. And Pervez hated letting down Shekhar with his script ideas.

'I will give it a think. Though I don't know what I can do to gain this experience.'

'Don't think so hard. Hurl yourself at unfamiliar things. Channelize those experiences of fear, disgust or delight into your writing. There is an interesting Experimental Theatre elective that's coming up in two weeks' time at the National School of Drama in New Delhi. Those students do the craziest things. I suggest you sign up for that course. It'll do you good.'

'Thanks, Shekhar. I really appreciate it. I have one last question for you.'

'Shoot.'

'You are obviously a sought-after writer and I have reason to believe that you are not much into fantasy either. What did you do to gain these experiences, as you call them?'

'I travelled with whatever money I had at my disposal. I put myself in uncomfortable scenarios. I went to Vietnam, lived and cooked there. I slept on floors when I had to. I waited at restaurants in the US when I had to make ends meet. And I still fell short, but yeah, that's what I did.'

'So, did you ever feel this pain you mention or the love that you spoke about?'

Shekhar hesitated for a moment. 'When my wife passed away last year, I think I felt it.'

Pervez knew this was a good time to stop.

Being in Shekhar's class was always an education. Meeting him one-on-one and listening to him was a pilgrimage. Pervez thanked Shekhar for his time once again. He was filled with inspiration. He had a month-long break coming up and the thought of travelling to an unknown city filled his senses with an unforeseen tinge of excitement.

His plan of having Rs 2,00,000 in the bank as a buffer for one year after FTII would get a definite jolt with any new plans, but he was ready to take a crack at it. First, he immediately signed up for the Experimental Theatre Course in New Delhi.

Second, he opened up a world map on his phone and charted out the nearest cities from India that he had never been to.

Three weeks later, Pervez was in downtown Shanghai without a clue in the world of how to navigate the busy metropolis. He had intentionally not crafted any itinerary except a visit to the Shanghai World Circus show, a ticket to which had been booked and was now lodged safely in his wallet.

Apart from a Google Translate app that came recommended from Ravin, one of his former hospitality-sector colleagues when he used to work with the Le Meridien and who had travelled to China before, Pervez chose to read nothing else about the city. Partly because before the summer break there were assignments to be completed and also because Pervez wanted to throw himself out in Shanghai and hopefully immerse himself in those uncomfortable experiences that Shekhar spoke to him about.

He was particularly looking forward to the World Circus show. Ravin had raved about it since the day Pervez mentioned his well-intentioned, but haphazard, trip to Shanghai. Ravin also gave a few handy suggestions about budget accommodations and street food delights. But most of all, he emphasized the Google Translate app.

'Shanghai is a modern metropolis but don't expect anyone there to know a word of English,' he cautioned Pervez. Ravin got Pervez to download a language pack that would work offline without Internet connectivity. Pervez realized the benefits of this as soon as he got into a cab at the Shanghai airport.

When the buck-toothed guy in a yellow cab asked him, *'Ni xiang qu nali?'*, not only was Pervez able to decipher that the driver wanted a destination, but in less than a minute he was able to read out from the language pack, *'Wo xiang qu Jin Jiang kezhan.'* (I want to go to Jin Jiang Inn.)

The hotel reception at Jin Jiang Inn had a similar experience in store for him, where once again his app came in handy. After settling into his budget hotel room, Pervez set out to do what any tourist would on a Shanghai evening— take a walk down the Bund.

The sight of the glittering buildings and their reflection in the calm waters soothed his eyes. His head, a little fuzzy after that rather long trip, needed this. He tried asking a few people for directions to Shanghai World Circus and realized Ravin's gift for this trip was invaluable. Without Google Translate, Pervez wouldn't be able to perhaps even feed himself.

His modest hotel had provided him with a map with the World Circus venue clearly circled on it. The balding receptionist indicated with his hands after much persuasion that it was a nine-kilometre walk from the Bund. Pervez, having budgeted two hours for the walk, started from the Bund at 7 p.m. towards Gonghe Xin Lu—the venue of the much-celebrated Shanghai World Circus.

On his walk, he encountered a bubbling energy that was exaggerated by the thousands of office-goers who were restless to return home. This buzz in the air of people walking busily with mobile phones, the resultant cacophony and the bright lights radiating from skyscrapers was a mélange unlike anything he had experienced.

While Pune and Gurgaon had people around busy areas, they also had large arid tracts that went on for miles without a person in sight. During his walk, he didn't encounter anything of the sort. It was a city bursting at the seams with people.

He reached the venue in under an hour-and-a-half. The set-up inside the massive oval auditorium was nothing impressive at first glance. While the ceiling extended really high, at the centre was a small circular elevated stage. An enormous wavy silk curtain hid everything else behind it. On it, a set of numbers that counted down to 9 p.m. ran in sync with a heavy ominous sound that thudded from the speakers.

Pervez took a sip of water from his bottle and hoped that the show would live up to its billing. He observed the people in the massive auditorium. Mostly, they consisted of tourist groups huddled together in different sections. There were a lot of couples and families too. The children especially had a sense of awe writ large on their faces.

Pervez was sitting on an aisle seat close to one of the exits, which he had specifically chosen bearing in mind that in case the show didn't impress him he could quietly make a retreat. There was a middle-aged family of three seated next to him.

The music had just started to build up when the man seated next to Pervez waved out to someone entering the auditorium. The other gentleman, an old man with teeth glossier than milk, waved at Pervez's neighbour fervently. He sauntered up to Pervez and spoke in a flurry of Mandarin.

Pervez, a little perplexed at the situation, wasn't sure what this man wanted as he furiously kept pointing to his ticket.

After a few seconds of tussle between Mandarin and English, Pervez understood that he was expected to volunteer his seat for another one a couple of rows ahead. Seeing that he didn't have much of a choice since the family of three also started speaking a little loudly, Pervez gave in. He exchanged his ticket with the old man and took his seat two rows ahead.

While watching the World Circus sandwiched between people wasn't Pervez's idea of spending time in a foreign city, he did notice that he had a very dignified neighbour on his left.

She must've been in her fifties and her salt-and-pepper hair was her most striking feature. Her thin nose and perfectly arranged hair were a dead giveaway that she was a native. Even in the cramped room that the seat gave her, she sat elegantly with her long legs crossed like a designer gracing the front row of a fashion show. In the few seconds in which he sized her up, he imagined her as a gazelle of a runner. Though dressed in a casual blue shirt and black trousers, she exuded beauty from her very being. Even without exchanging any words, Pervez felt overawed.

A loud trumpet-like sound indicated the show was all set to begin. To relax himself, Pervez leaned back in his seat. The moment he did that, he caught a waft of the most intoxicating fragrance in the world as the tall lady turned her head towards Pervez and smiled. He smiled back.

The circus for the next one hour featured some of the most nail-biting stunts that Pervez had ever seen. Large rounds of applause rang in after every ten minutes as the performers— some of the best-looking oriental men and women—put their lives on the line to perform gravity-defying acrobatics to the audience's delight.

As the show neared its end, a large barrel-shaped wooden circle that hung from the ceiling was lowered further on to the main stage. It looked like the Wall of Death motorcycling stunts that Pervez had seen as a child in some of the carnivals back in New Delhi. This specific cylinder, however, was imposing.

The first set of three bikers arrived and started riding along the perimeter of the circle to a pulsating music set. It wasn't anything special yet and Pervez wondered why a famous circle troupe would close a terrific show with such an old, commonplace stunt. The audience, however, perhaps knew better as they started cheering for the three bikers.

The music picked up beat, as out of the blue three new bikers entered the circle from the top of the ceiling. The audience cheered wildly. To have six bikers in that space was a little maddening to watch, and they didn't just follow a straight route. They swerved in different directions in the blink of an eye. Clearly, this was way better than what Pervez thought would be the finale and he began enjoying this a lot more. He joined in instinctively, clapping his hands in tandem with the rest of the audience.

And right then another set of three bikers entered without notice. There was a collective gasp from the audience. This was unthinkable. Pervez involuntarily threw his head back in a burst of surprise. It was all happening so fast and that constant whirring sound only made it the most thrilling experience in the world. He immediately felt someone grabbing at his wrist. It was his neighbour.

She couldn't bear to watch this bit. She had turned her face away from the scene of the action and buried it in Pervez's left shoulder. While this motorcycle stunt was the most jaw-dropping thing Pervez had ever seen, it was her proximity to Pervez and her touch that made him feel like an ounce of butter melting away. He didn't quite know what to do but instinctively placed his hand over hers. Her hands felt so soft, but all he could hear now were her heavy sighs.

She sat like that for the next few seconds until the sound of the bikes were overpowered by the thunderous applause of the crowd. By then, her breath had settled into a normal rhythm but Pervez wanted time to stand still. As she lifted her head, their eyes met. Pervez felt a rush of blood in his head. Their pulses now beat in perfect rhythm. She looked at him for what seemed like an eternity until she realized that the two of them were the only ones sitting in an auditorium of thousands of people, all of whom had risen to give the World Circus team a standing ovation.

The elegant lady and Pervez eventually joined in, albeit a couple of moments later.

All the performers came on to the stage and acknowledged the cheers that were reserved for them. As the people exited, they couldn't stop talking to each other in admiration. One didn't need to understand the language to appreciate the sense of wonderment that pervaded the air. Pervez and his neighbour walked out, matching their steps, yet not a single word was spoken.

Near the exit, Pervez and the lady found themselves being squished among the others who were trying to make a quick getaway. Pervez summed up all the courage he had to hold her hand and keep her by his side as they found their way out to the main road. To Pervez, her palm belied her age. It felt as soft as a toddler's. All this while, she kept her head bowed.

The street by now had completely transformed. A milieu of vendors, in anticipation of the crowd, had lined up with stalls of all kinds of merchandise and street food. Bright and shiny fridge magnets, T-shirts and mugs coexisted alongside freshly roasted shrimp and beef baos. Every inch of space outside the auditorium was invaded by vendors.

Pervez and his lady companion turned the other way and walked through a couple of busy alleys for the next ten minutes. There was still mayhem on these roads with taxis wheeling in and out in the hope of some late-night surge business.

In this noise, with both of them holding each other's hand, Pervez wondered what might be a good topic for starting a conversation. Should he ask her if she knew English? But would that be a better start than him trying to initiate conversation in Chinese? That should crack her up. Never a bad start. His head was going berserk with these questions as they continued to walk through the lanes. He was only here for a week and there was so much to go over with her.

They reached a slightly quieter lane and Pervez playfully pressed her index finger. She looked at him and responded with a more pronounced grasp on his hand.

The script of Pervez's first night in Shanghai couldn't have been written better. Just then his eye caught the signage of a restaurant called Blue Frog. This was one of the restaurants that Ravin had recommended. Being the only one on the list with an English name, it was neatly painted in Pervez's memory. Pervez looked at the lady on his right for her approval, which he got in an instant.

They occupied a table near the kitchen. Pervez let out a smile and said slowly, 'I a . . . m . . . P . . . e . . . r . . . v . . . e . . . z.' . He finally took out his mobile phone and showed her the Google Translate app. 'I h . . . a . . .v . . . e Mandarin language o . . . n . . . this . . . Y . . . o . . . u have Goo . . . gle or . . . Or B . . . ai . . . du . . . ?'

She broke into a laugh that was full of life. These were peals of delight that filled the little private space Pervez shared with this elegant lady in this jam-packed restaurant.

'I don't know Mandarin. But I can learn. I am a quick learner,' he said, excited.

She took both her hands to her lips as if she were making a sign of a kiss. And then held them a little away. She then made a gesture to mean that she didn't know how to speak. It took a second for Pervez to gather that it was not because she didn't want to. It was because she couldn't.

As Pervez kept the phone aside, he felt that searing pain that Prof. Apte had referred to. It resulted from a woman he had barely shared a laugh with, but one he could've waged a war for.

This story is inspired by the travels of a journalist friend who, for a week, roamed around Hangzhou and Guangzhou in the company of a native female Chinese companion with a fully charged mobile phone and the Google Translate offline pack.

An Offer to Remember

After graduating from the National School of Drama, Debbie Malhotra was torn between acting and writing as a career. It would be a while before either of those professions started paying the bills.

But there was another form of writing emerging furiously in the Indian content creation scene and that was to create lists such as, 'Top ten reasons why this summer is bad for your pimples,' or 'Watch out for these eight things to find out if your boyfriend is eating too much mayo.' This form of writing, while unintelligent and facetious, could be a good way to rake in the moolah, she figured.

Debbie knew little about the various players in this industry that relied solely on talent to write click-baity headlines and generate regaling memes day after day. But a friend told her that on top of this pile of companies that competed daily to generate between themselves anywhere between 100 videos and 200 articles a day, there reigned a company called Yours Virally.

And that's how on a Monday morning, Debbie found herself in the office of Yours Virally in Andheri West. The editor, Subhashish, had called her in for a meeting after seeing some of her writing samples. Now she was told that he was delayed by an hour.

Debbie, who had recently been on a series of misfired dates through Tinder, thought nothing of opening the app during daylight hours at an office reception to kill time.

The first few profiles were easy choices to be swiped to the left. The sixth one that emerged had a crowning description to go with a handsome picture. The name was Riz Khan and the description went:

I am a man of many seasons. Some that withered away, some that are yet to bloom. Presently, I teach, formerly an assassin in the Army.

When she snooped around a little for pictures on Riz's Tinder profile, apart from his bearded face that would've found a place in the pantheon of Greek Gods, she saw a Calvin quote, a picture of Riz in an Arsenal jersey and another picture where he stood next to Margaret Atwood.

She peered into the last picture with special interest and ascertained that this wasn't a photoshopped picture. Next, she pinched herself and went to her own profile description:

I am a writer in conflict living as an actress in distress. I get through each day because of all things Calvin, Arsenal and Margaret Atwood.

This was too good to be true and it knocked the wind out of her. So much so that she was convinced that Riz was an apparition. Being around him or hoping to hear back from him would be nothing short of a disaster.

No sooner had she swiped right on Riz, than she regretted it. Tinder had an option to go back and unselect your previous option. A thing this perfect could only land her in misery, her depressed writing mind rationalized. As she was about to unselect Riz, she received a pop-up. It read 'Perfect match'. A message from Riz followed.

Riz: *My flight's about to take off. I only have an hour before I leave Mumbai for good, but is this really happening?*

Debbie: *I knew it. Something had to be wrong about this.*

Riz: *Let me call you. Ping me your number here.*

Debbie: *No, not right now. What if I am too disappointing for you to have a last unhappy memory of Mumbai.*

Riz: *I see we have a drama queen here.*

Debbie: *Since everyone would ask you how you met Margaret Atwood, I am going to be a little different . . .*

Riz: *You recognized Margaret Atwood in a picture? You're a keeper!*

Debbie: *Who wouldn't! You don't tend to attract blind people, do you?*

Riz: *I don't know. No one's ever caught that. I had a picture with Al Pacino and everyone was raving about it.*

Debbie: *Now you are showing off . . .*

Riz: *No, I was only bartending back then. Nothing to show off. It's not as if I acted with him.*

Debbie: *So, teacher, assassin and a bartender. How come?*

Riz: *I was undercover when I was bartending. And teacher because nothing happens when you are undercover, so I had to do something.*

Debbie: *Tell me the Margaret Atwood story.*

Riz: *Met her at a dinner. Was a launch event for a book a colleague had written.*

Debbie: *What was she like?*

Riz: *In one word. Sassy. In two words. Very sassy.*

Debbie: *I want to kill you and then go back in time undercover as you.*

Riz: *What's your story?*

Debbie: *Lifelong theatre addict. Master's in contemporary theatre from NSD, Delhi, landed in Mumbai this morning for an interview. And now thinking should've done something else.*

Riz: *Favourite playwright?*

Debbie: *Oscar Wilde and David Mamet. Between them, they've all genres covered. Yours?*

Riz: *I don't have any. I only asked the question so I would sound sophisticated and artistic.*

Debbie: *Are you always this honest?*

Riz: *No, I never mention that I am married on Tinder.*

For the next ten seconds, Debbie wasn't sure what to type.

Riz was used to this. Most women were stumped to find a married man on Tinder.

Riz: *I know you want to ask what I am doing on this app if I am married.*

Debbie: *No, I couldn't care less. You are leaving anyway. What good will come of this?*

Riz: *That's a good note to begin a conversation with a stranger. By writing it off from the get go.*

Debbie: *Don't put it on me. But pray tell why you are on the app if you are married?*

Riz: *My wife and I are looking for a partner for a threesome.*

Debbie: *I am out. Was nice knowing you.*

Debbie wanted to unmatch Riz. But this conversation had a bite to it that she wanted more of. She delayed the thought of unmatching him for ten seconds and closed her eyes and took deep breaths.

The receptionist, a frail chalk-haired woman, wondered if Debbie was well. She had seen many an interviewee become nervous here in the lobby, but these deep breaths were a first.

What Riz said next calmed her nerves further.

Riz: *No, silly! I am kidding. About the threesome, not about the wedding.*

Debbie: *Why do married men do this?*

Riz: *I don't know about others . . .*

Debbie: *But?*

Riz: *Long story. I have only ten minutes before I take off.*

Debbie: *Shoot.*

Debbie sees Riz typing something for the next ten seconds and no message comes forth.

Debbie: *What are you doing? Type fast. You are on a tight leash on time.*

Riz: *Hold on, getting into the plane. Dropped my handbag.*

Debbie: *Ooh, did anyone find out about the bomb?*

Riz: *Oh, move on with the stereotypes. Give me a minute.*

Riz: *I am on the app for a distracting conversation, that's it.*

Debbie: *And why are you leaving town?*

Riz: *To begin this life on a new note.*

Debbie: *And what is this new note?*

Riz: *Setting up a small farm in Mussoorie to grow mushrooms.*

Debbie: *You aren't serious?*

Riz: *I am. Nobody in India grows good mushrooms. I am going to change that and supply it to restaurants in Mumbai.*

Debbie: *And your wife is moving with you?*

Riz: *No, she manages a big business here. We are going to be long distance for some time. Most likely, she will stay in Mumbai.*

Debbie: *Now it all makes sense. You are using Tinder as your fail-safe option.*

Riz: *I object. I just wanted to have a good old extra-marital fling. Not looking for a fail-safe option.*

Debbie: *A fling, huh? Again, full marks for honesty. Why did you swipe on me?*

Riz: *Your curls.*

Debbie: *My curls? That's all you have to say to a twenty-three-year-old who is not judging you for being married?*

Riz: *Well, you did judge me when I said threesome.*

Debbie: *Everyone has their threshold levels. Shouldn't they? Why would I ever hook up with a stranger couple. What if you guys are ex-convicts who will drug-rape me.*

Riz: *Why did you swipe?*

Debbie: *You have pictures of the three things that help me get through life. Have you even read my profile? Or did you not go beyond my curls?*

Riz: *It was uncanny. Don't remind me. What are the fucking odds? I feel like getting off the plane just in case it crashes and I never get to meet you.*

Debbie: *Hold your horses. Who said anything about a meeting?*

Riz: *But can you imagine, we are both like . . .*

Debbie: *Do you wanna say siblings?*

Riz: *Fuck you. You are a killjoy, you know that right?*

Riz: *But you know what I mean. This is a one-in-a-million kind of a thing. We should meet just to get to know each other better. Nothing more, nothing less.*

Debbie: *I am not opposed to meeting. But pray tell how if you are moving to another city. And I am not even from Mumbai. I don't even know if I am going to move here.*

Riz: *Why do you 'pray tell' so much?*

Debbie: *Blame it on the English drama dialogue I read in college.*

Riz: *Where are you from?*

Debbie: *New Delhi.*

Riz: *Well, Mussoorie is not far from New Delhi. It's closer than Mumbai, if you know what I mean.*

Debbie: *I don't know what you mean. Is that what we are gonna count on now? Miles?*

Riz: *As an aside, normally I would get unmatched within seconds of telling people that I am married. Why haven't you unmatched me yet?*

Debbie: *Why do you keep telling people that you are married?*

Riz: *All I want to do is have a distracting conversation and nothing else. I would rather be honest about it.*

Debbie: *Are you sure about the nothing else?*

Riz: *Honestly? Not so much.*

Debbie: *There you go. I knew it.*

Riz: *So, I shouldn't be doing this?*

Debbie: *Not my place to suggest. Wait, give me a minute.*

Riz: *Why? What happened? Remember I am on a clock here. I could be gone by the time you come back to this futile conversation.*

Debbie: *It's worth the futility. The receptionist wants to talk. I don't want to let go of you yet. Will take two minutes and be back. Don't fly yet.*

Riz: *It's not like I am the one flying this plane. Though I do know how to fly one.*

Debbie: *Just when I thought you couldn't be more perfect.*

Riz: *Just when I thought I really should get off the plane and come and fetch you.*

The receptionist informed Debbie that the creative director might not be able to make it today at all and that she was trying to get an interview arranged with the CEO.

'How long before you can confirm this?' Debbie asked.

'In half an hour. Our CEO is just getting done from a meeting. I can ask her in person.'

Debbie returned to her chat.

Debbie: *Here I am.*

Riz: *What interview are you giving?*

Debbie: *This company called Yours Virally. The CEO is in a meeting. The receptionist will tell me in half an hour if she can meet with me. Heard of the company?*

Riz: *Hell yeah!*

Debbie: *Relax, why the extra energy all of a sudden?*

Riz: *My wife is the CEO. You are in the Andheri office?*

Debbie read that twice.

Debbie: *Please tell me you are kidding. That would make this ridiculous. And I can sense a panic attack coming. I can't take this.*

Riz: *Panic attack?*

Debbie: *I have my moments. I don't want to screw up this interview knowing that I just chatted, wait, 'plotted' to have a scene with her husband.*

Riz: *Were you?*

Debbie: *Were you what?*

Riz: *Thinking of having a scene with me? What does a 'scene' mean anyway for people of your generation?*

Debbie: *It could mean a lot of things. But first, is this woman your wife? I don't even know her name. I wasn't even supposed to meet her. Wait, I need some water.*

Debbie emptied half a bottle of water kept nearby and started panting as she typed. The receptionist raised her eyebrows again.

Debbie: *I need to lie down. I can't believe I decided to go to Tinder while waiting for an interview. Worst. Decision. Ever. I can't do this.*

Riz: *I am serious. But what work will you have with her anyway? I don't think she will meet you for an interview. She only interviews business guys.*

Debbie's heart pounded. She needed this job so badly. She looked for the Xanax pills her doctor had prescribed in her purse. It was the worst day to leave them behind.

Debbie: *I think I am fainting. At least give me some tips. Something, anything.*

Riz: *She will ask you for a personal example of grit and determination. Not in your professional life but in your personal life. It's important to her.*

Debbie: *I don't trust you. What's her name?*

Riz: *And then there's this one question that she asks everyone and that is the clinching question for her.*

Debbie: *What is it?*

Riz: *My flight's taking off.*

Debbie: *Don't do this. Stop the damn thing. I forgot my pills too. I can't believe it. WHAT'S THE QUESTION?*

Riz: *She will ask you . . . if . . .*

Debbie: *If WHAT*

Riz: *If you ever chatted with Riz on Tinder . . .*

Debbie felt like smashing his head.

Debbie: *I can't believe you are taking this so lightly. Please tell me you were kidding.*

Riz: *I am used to freaking people out with the information they give me. Like I only knew that Yours Virally is based out of Andheri and . . .*

Debbie: *Go away. Just go! I am not talking to you.*

Riz: *You are wrecked right now, aren't you?*

Debbie: *Of course, I am. I have had anxiety attacks where I faint. This was way too close and I hate you for it. That's also why I chose to become a writer and not an actor.*

Riz: *Did you know Emma Stone overcame panic attacks and made it this big?*

Debbie: *You like Emma Stone?*

Riz: *She's celestial.*

Debbie: *You are killing me. She's my favourite actress. Why do we both like the exact same things! Anyway, I think I am gonna faint and lose this job.*

Riz: *It's exactly that, just a job. There'll be another one waiting if you don't get this. But . . .*

Debbie: *But what?*

Riz: *But if we don't agree to meet during the course of this conversation, will we ever find someone with this level of connection again?*

Debbie: *Easy for you to say. I need this job. I don't have a rich father who will allow me to grow mushrooms. In fact, I don't even have a father. But I do feel the need to meet you too.*

Riz: *I get it. You don't worry about it too much. You will do fine. Time for me to leave.*

Debbie: *But let me put it out there blunt and clear.*

Riz: *What?*

Debbie: *I WANT to meet you whenever you are back in Mumbai next. Call me.*

Riz: *I will. And good luck for the interview.*

Half an hour later, the receptionist informed Debbie that the interview had been scheduled. The CEO, Abha Kapoor, turned out to be a genial lady in her forties, who skimmed through her resume and read one of the writing samples Debbie had placed in front of her.

'You write well, but this is not the sort of writing that we have on our website. If you know what I mean,' Abha said.

'I know, but given a brief I can put together any number of lists, especially around topics of films and theatre, which are my forte,' Debbie said calmly.

'Subhashish, our creative director, couldn't be here because he had to attend to a medical emergency in the morning. He would be best placed to take a call on your candidature. But before you go, could you give me a couple of personal examples of grit and determination?'

Right then, Debbie fainted out of exertion and the genial Abha Kapoor, out of sheer pity for the poor girl, rolled out an appointment letter later that evening. Debbie got to know that Abha had never married, but Riz's sense of humour didn't go down well with her and she promptly unmatched him.

That evening Maya, Riz's wife, asked him, 'Did you manage to find someone today?'

'No, I was close to meeting a gullible young girl but something ticked her off. Can't put a finger on what it was. She unmatched me in the evening,' he said.

Maya calmly said, 'I'll tell you. You need to put a lid on your sense of humour. My turn tomorrow. We better find a partner soon to spice things up between us.'

They turned their backs to each other and went to sleep.

Table for One

'Sir, I need you to step aside for a moment,' the skinny, grey-haired John, manager of Khwaaish, the hot new restaurant on Waterfield Road, said to Akshay.

Akshay Karmakar was not the kind of guy you would ask to step aside while he was waiting for his meal. The man was big. At the same time, he was radically polite. 'Oh sure, would you like to join me?'

'No,' said John.

'Can we do this after I dig into my Khwaaish-e-Nalli?'

'No, sorry. You have to come with me now.'

'But why?'

'Because this is the second time this month that you have called in with a reservation for a table of four. May I ask where the rest of your party is?'

'They are on their way. They should be here in fifteen at best,' Akshay pushed his chair to get up. It was going to take more than a moment.

'I know all about you, Akshay Karmakar. You either come with me now or I am going to have to call security.'

There was not much to know about Akshay Karmakar. Except that ever since he separated from his wife, Rashi, four years ago, he went from a svelte 62 kg to a hefty 94 kg.

There was not much on offer for reclusive, obese and separated men on the dating front in Mumbai. Besides, being brought up in an orphanage meant that he never had any friends to fall back on. He also never got to know about the fate of his parents. He stayed alone, studied alone and ate alone these past few years after his separation.

Eating out served as an easy delusional escape for Akshay who had also, just before his separation, lost his job at Lester Brothers as they had gone bankrupt. In urban cities around the world, a rising trend that was seen among separated couples was a phenomenon called the Revenge Body—a term that described a person's ambition for a physically fit body after a break-up. It wouldn't be unfair to say that Akshay single-handedly demolished the sheer notion of that phenomenon with his revenge eating.

He loved his food so much that every year he would look at the Best Restaurants that *Time Out* Mumbai listed. Then he would compare it to TripAdvisor's top-rated restaurants and cross-reference it with India's *Michelin Guide*.

After this, he would spend a couple of days with his whiteboard and blue marker to studiously curate a list of restaurants he would like to visit over the course of the year. This had been Akshay Karmakar's Christmas holiday plan for the last three years. The first time he embarked on this journey was with his wife back in 2011. Back then, you didn't even have to make a call to visit a restaurant and book a table, but 2016 turned out to be a beast in this regard.

People were reading these informed reviews more than ever. They were hijacking the same phone numbers off the likes of Zomato and accessing the same websites to make these bookings. Where Akshay realized he was missing out was that he only needed a table for one. Most of the time, these fancy restaurants gave preference to reservations for two or more for better business and consigned tables for one to a doomed waiting list. That list might as well have been called Waiting for Godot, for the ones waiting for a Table for One were never allocated a seat.

Post New Year's, a downturn of dining out invariably hit Mumbai. That's when Akshay would scour the web and make those painful calls or click on those grids of dates on online websites of restaurants to reserve his table. It worked every year since he started this practice in 2012. Being a nerd with an opinion about the latest on Mumbai's dining circuit gave Akshay the only shred of social legitimacy in his pedantic life.

That's when he came up with a simple hack to veer away from those waiting lists.

Akshay tried his luck first with Chutney Mary by booking a table for four. He then followed it up with a booking for two at The Sushi Tetsu. It worked. He would get seated and when asked about the rest of the party, he would simply say, 'They are on their way.'

'Would you like to wait or order now?' the staff would ask him.

'I think I'll go ahead,' Akshay would answer with a twinkle in his eyes. And there the matter would rest.

This was in February. Over the next couple of months, he was able to follow the same procedure and get his tables a tad easily than before. It was still tough, but his strike rate improved marginally.

Akshay wasn't rich enough to dine out every week. He would save up to have two world-class meals a month. That was his singular goal. And the new restaurants came galloping every month. After every meal, he would studiously write a review for TripAdvisor, which was nothing less than a meticulously constructed opera in honour of the food.

Maybe he stretched his luck at Khwaaish. But he was too tempted. The tasting menu was out of this world. That Nalli Sunahri he had at the beginning of the month was still fresh in his mind. He wanted to come here again so badly.

But he made one mistake. He booked a table for four for the second time in less than a month at Khwaaish. Thrice, on each occasion, the waiting staff inquired about the rest of his party. Each time Akshay shrugged his shoulders and told them that the others were going to be late.

The first time this month at Khwaaish, a placid, fulfilled Akshay looked at John and said, 'I'll take the cheque. Too bad the others missed the meal. Mumbai traffic and its horrors.'

But John was only too mindful about the faces walking into the restaurant. It struck him then that Akshay's party of four never arrived. He let it pass. Akshay had also left a generous tip for the staff. It was a fine modus operandi that worked across the spring of 2016 till John came by his table today.

Akshay stood up in the only way he could. Slowly.

'I know it looks like a coincidence because it's the second time,' Akshay spluttered. 'But what can you say about my friends. So errant,' he rued.

'Why don't you save yourself the time and the trouble Mr Karmakar?'

'You know what, I will step aside and call them again. It's no trouble.'

For fancy restaurants like Khwaaish, saving time amounted to earning money and John was only being the ever-so-diligent guardsman for his restaurant.

'Can someone please call the security?' a cold John blurted emphatically, standing in the middle of Khwaaish, protecting his turf from this unscrupulous soul.

All the distinguished gentlemen and elegant ladies, with their shining cutlery mid-air, froze in their seats. The rhythm of the knives and forks on the other tables thawed.

By now, Akshay knew there was no point continuing the gag any further. Two security guards came in and stood next to him.

'There's no need. Save it,' Akshay said, dropping his napkin on the floor.

His succulent Khwaaish-e-Nalli had just arrived and the delicious aroma of the visibly soft lamb had assailed his senses already. But it was time to let dignity win one round over gluttony for the moment.

At the exit, an elderly couple looked at Akshay with disgust. 'Do you think he stole something from here?' the lady asked dipping into her orange blossom cake with strained yoghurt that Akshay recognized from his last visit here.

'Look at him, the chav! I bet he couldn't pay for his meal.'

More than John acting like a complete jackass, it was this comment that stung Akshay Karmakar. He went home wanting to never have another meal again outside of his basement apartment in Mulund.

Akshay earned an honest buck and was spending it well within his means for a decent meal. Did any of the others in the restaurant ever win the title of Gold Reviewer bestowed by TripAdvisor to a hand-picked few every year? Could they ever verbalize the intricacies of spice and flavour? Did the rich really know their food or did they come to these restaurants because it gave them a reason to click a picture for their social media profiles?

Akshay opened his laptop and did what he did best: spend time with the latest version of Grand Theft Auto. But these questions hovered over the noise of his on-screen Porsche. He was many things—a smart liar, or even a crook with a hungry soul, but not a chav. Please! That comment from the old couple still rankled in his ears.

He wanted to hit back at Khwaaish. Once he channelized his energies towards that end, he spent the next half an hour putting together a note.

'Despicable, disgusting food. Think before you barf here, let alone eat.'

This place is surviving on a short-lived legacy of a few good reviews garnered in its initial days. Let me paint you the real story. Because right now the food is so bad, I suppose an unborn infant could cook better than what I was served. The Amritsari Basa was so chewy, you might be better off chewing gum instead. Oh, and the pulled duck breast, so raw that the poor animal was perhaps still breathing when he was served on my plate. I would shudder before I go anywhere near Khwaaish in the near future.

I am convinced all these five reviews posted before mine were from people who were paid by Khwaaish to post good reviews. You know the drill.

I would give this deplorable shanty a negative hundred on a scale of one to five. It's a pity you can't do that here on TripAdvisor.

Akshay felt his spirit renew as he wrote this short note and posted it on TripAdvisor. The average rating for the place was 4.4. But since it was a new restaurant, he knew that with his damning review he would have a big impact in pulling down the rating for Khwaaish.

By the time he woke up, two people had already marked his review helpful.

'That's interesting,' he muttered to himself.

And then he came up with a thought far viler than the act of posting a false review.

'What if I created ten fake profiles and posted terrible reviews through them on TripAdvisor. That would take Khwaaish down entirely,' he ruminated.

That would require a lot of work. But Akshay was no stranger to organizing his thoughts on a whiteboard and following it through. At best, it would take a weekend away from him. But a string of negative reviews could irreparably dent Khwaaish, he mused.

His plan made, Akshay went off to sleep soundly.

The next morning, he had another ping on the TripAdvisor rating. Never before had his phone pinged so early on a weekend. On weekdays of course, troubles from all over JP Morgan's global offices would land in his inbox.

He opened his TripAdvisor profile eagerly. It was a reply to his review. It read:

This is John, Restaurant Manager, Khwaaish

I am disappointed to read this review from Akshay. If anything, this is symptomatic of the kind of trolling that service businesses like ours deal with on a daily basis.

Akshay called in earlier this month asking for a table for four. On the appointed date and time, he came alone. He mentioned his friends were running late. Yesterday, he did the exact same thing. When we politely asked him to leave, he gave us the exact same excuse.

As a busy restaurant, we are sometimes constrained to give preferences to larger parties while giving reservations. Even then, we place all individual requests on our waiting lists.

I can only imagine that Akshay's desperation, when he didn't find a table at our restaurant, drove him to make a false booking for a table for four. Not once, but twice.

From our security cameras we have shared a picture of his with the Bombay Restaurant Association, so that people like Akshay cannot simply walk over the hard-working people of our industry. We have agreed jointly, as of yesterday, to bar him from entering any of the member restaurants.

I urge you to not judge us based on this single, extremely biased review. Visit us and see for yourself the wonderful hospitality that Khwaaish has to offer.

One last thing, as proof, mentioned below is the feedback that Akshay left for us on a physical form the last time he was here. He rated us 5 on ambience and service. About the food, Akshay had left a hand-written note saying, 'I would give you a 100 on a scale of 5. Pity, you don't give me the option.' Attached is the screenshot.'

Akshay felt something inside while reading this—like someone had run amok stomping his gut from within.

What was this Bombay Restaurant Association that he didn't know about? The thought of him possibly not getting an entry into any of the other fancy restaurants shook the very foundations of his tasting buds. What about the bookings for next month at The Manor and Pali Bhavan Panchayat?

He didn't have to wait long to find out. By afternoon, he had a mail from each of them stating that he was being denied reservation request on technical grounds.

Akshay spent the next few days brooding about the fate of his culinary delights. What was he going to do? Would pubs open themselves to him? And who are the members of this sinister Bombay Restaurant Association? What if he was humiliated in some unforeseen manner if he stepped inside a restaurant again?

Will this ban ever be lifted off him? Should he move cities?

JP Morgan was a large company and they could place him in Delhi or Pune if he placed a request. His skills were secular as a professional; he could employ them anywhere.

Sipping a beer later that week, in a faraway rundown drinking hole in Thane, Akshay decided to put in a request to be transferred. He didn't want to leave his beloved Maharashtra. But Pune would be a nice change. It's not as if he was leaving behind much in Mumbai. There was no one and nothing to leave behind.

The time was nigh for a complete reboot.

Akshay was convinced that starting a new life all over again meant disassociating from every digital trace of his life as well. He decided to delete his Facebook account to which the TripAdvisor reviews were linked.

He went home that day with a faint hope of a new life. He logged into his Facebook account and looked at all his old status posts. Most of them were a cynical view of the world, but he also praised some of the best dishes in Mumbai.

Before this wave of fancy dinners in recent years, he was quite the street-farer. He smiled to himself reading his short critiques about the spiced vada-pavs from Dadar, the mirchi bhajia at Mulund, or the handmade cotton candies near Borivali National Park on his profile.

Among the ninety-three friends he had, he would often hear from them about those street food reviews. Because this food was what all those friends of his could afford.

Lately, he had started using words like plating and delectable on his food review posts. Fewer friends now liked or commented on these posts. 'When did I start caring about plating,' he wondered.

Maybe there is a future for him in street food in Pune. Maybe he went overboard in this pursuit of fine dining. Maybe there was a way for him to survive in Mumbai by simply going back to the food that he tasted from these streets.

But nothing was going to stop him from deleting his Facebook account. His new life wouldn't start until he struck out every past digital remnant of his life.

He looked out for the delete profile button. As he went through all his recent and old messages, he observed that under filtered requests he had one unread message. He opened it. It was from one Nikhila.

Hi Akshay, this is Nikhila here. I feel odd writing to you like this. But I read John's message on that TripAdvisor review of yours and couldn't resist looking you up here.

I wanted to let you know that I completely empathize with your situation and must confess that I have myself booked larger tables as a cover since I often eat alone in this city. I don't think these people realize how single people like you and I find it difficult to get a table for one at good restaurants.

Well, if you ever want to step out together, let me know and we could at least book a table for two and look more respectable. My number is 8453002595.

Speak soon. Bye!

Akshay read that mail a zillion times and composed himself before framing a reply. He looked at her profile. She was a vision in an airline uniform, working as an air hostess perhaps. It wasn't very clear from her profile but she had lots of pictures taken at airports around the world.

He found her pigtails charming. That alone merited a reply.

Hey Nikhila,

So glad to hear from one of our tribe. How about we start from a place where we won't have to worry about reserving a table? I hear the good old chaat near Mithibai College is still as great. Fancy a meeting there next week? Take care, Akshay.

He had reason to give Mumbai one more chance.

Once, in a restaurant in Indiranagar, my wife and I were given a table ahead of a gentleman who was waiting before us. It took me back to my days of solitary dining in Mumbai. I always had a longer wait than anyone walking in with a partner or friends.

Home Delivered

'I had specifically mentioned an extra helping of coriander chutney along with the mint chutney,' said Zubin with a touch of anxiety and anger. The restraint in his voice was typical of a hard-working man in his late thirties.

'Sorry, sir. We didn't get any such instruction,' the voice at the other end of the line croaked.

'It's there alongside the order section in the app where you ask if there are extra directions for the food. Why do you have it in there if nobody reads that section?'

But Zubin knew that the damage to his dinner was irreparable. By the time anyone would even send him the chutney, his freshly cooked Lucknowi chicken tikka roll would lose its sheen. There was no point getting riled. He sat on his leather couch, turned on Netflix and bit into the succulent fare in front of him, albeit without the coriander chutney he so desired.

He comforted himself with the thought that his next meal would be better. Having a good meal was like having a steady companion by your side in an insular city like Mumbai. The barrage of food-ordering apps made it that much easier for bachelors and spinsters to believe that their late evenings had been put to good use.

The next morning, the whiff of the missed coriander chutney hammered Zubin's senses at work. He got through the day with the sole intention of ordering that delicious chicken tikka roll once again from Khwaaish, that hot new restaurant that had recently started delivering through Tiny Owl.

Zubin also thought of a workaround to plug the loophole that laid him bereft of the coriander chutney on his plate the previous evening. The mundane events of the day, however, took longer than anticipated. In the evening, Zubin found himself racing against time to place an order for the Lucknowi chicken tikka roll.

Right after he placed his order at 9.30 p.m. on the app, he frantically called and asked for the restaurant manager at Khwaaish.

'John, hi, I am Zubin. I frequently order from your restaurant. I am flat number A–104 from the Rustomjee Towers. I have just placed an order for two Lucknowi chicken tikka rolls through Tiny Owl.'

'Thank you for your patronage, sir. How can we help you?' a cold voice addressed Zubin.

'I needed some coriander chutney with the roll. I had requested for the same last night as well, but for some reason it never came.'

'Might have been the chef's decision, sir, because that's not how the chef intended for the roll to be eaten. We give it with the mint chutney because it soothes the marination on the soft meat of the pullet.'

'No, I don't mean to mess with the intended recipe. It's just that I wanted the coriander chutney as well.'

'I am not sure we can do that, sir.'

'Why not? I can pay extra.'

'It's not a matter of extra money, sir. It is about the artistic integrity of our food.'

'Goddamn you, you p****. Give me what I want or I will shoot you in the eye' was the first sentence that blitzed past Zubin's head but that Parsi restraint was at work again in a classy way.

'It's for my five-year-old daughter. I am a chef myself and I know what you mean, but my kid is particularly fond of that coriander chutney you serve. You will make a young girl very happy if you do this, John. I implore you.'

There are better sob stories in this world. But for a busy man like John, this was good enough. 'Sure, sir. I understand. What mobile number did you order from? I will get it done,' an impassive John relented.

Zubin got home just in time for the order. The first thing he did was to check if the green coriander chutney was in place. His wandering right hand settled on two transparent twin sachets that were the exact colour he was looking for. With a celebratory fist pump, Zubin marvelled at civilization's acceptance of lies woven around children, sat on his leather couch, turned on Netflix and unpacked the rolls.

There was one tiny problem though. They smelt nothing like chicken. And they definitely didn't feel like that pullet John referred to. Zubin fumed.

If there's one thing he hated more than not having the right accompanying sauce for his dinner, it was paneer. Being lactose intolerant, Zubin couldn't stand paneer. And here he was holding in his plate a pair of paneer *bhurji* rolls, with the green chutney lying in wait like a nubile virgin.

He called the delivery boy. It took some time to explain the specific situation at hand.

'Sir, I am sorry. I must've given your order to the madam above yours. I was carrying both those orders.

I will come back and get this sorted, sir,' the delivery boy acknowledged.

'Which madam?'

'The one in A–204. Above yours. She just called me to tell me that her order was wrong. I am already on my way, sir. Should be there in ten minutes.'

'No, it's okay. I will go up,' Zubin said, his hunger turning into a steady wail from within.

He slipped into a pair of jeans while cursing the food delivery guy for doing this to him tonight. It was a constant battle with these delivery guys. Sometimes it was about the address, sometimes about the accompaniments and now the latest, the mixed-up order.

He quickly climbed up the stairs to find the right apartment.

It had been six years since Zubin was staying in this apartment block, but this was the first time he was going to speak to anyone in the building. Holding the paneer rolls in one hand, he rang the bell. His legs were shaking involuntarily, thinking about his delicious dinner that was held captive on the other side of this door.

The sound of a reluctant latch going back and forth from inside sharpened his yearning. He could hear someone trying to open the door. After what seemed like an eternity, a tall lady with a beautifully sun-tanned face emerged. Her white Star Wars T-shirt was appropriate for the occasion for she did seem otherworldly.

'Sorry to keep you waiting. I am still getting used to this door,' she said.

'Oh, no problem. Umm . . . I am here because the delivery guy mixed up our order. Did you order the paneer rolls from Khwaaish by any chance?'

'Yes, I did. I was wondering what happened and I even called the guy. But I was so hungry that I started eating those chicken rolls. Is that *my* order there?' she said, looking at the packet in Zubin's hands.

'How could you eat those chicken rolls? It wasn't even *your* order!' Zubin wanted to scream but again, that Parsi restraint rose like a phoenix.

'Yes, I thought just in case you were a vegetarian, I should return them,' he said half-convincingly. His eyes darted towards her right hand which was soaked in that familiar marinade of those rolls he so wanted to have tonight.

'I am so sorry! I am Malvika by the way. Please come in.'

Since she said she had started eating those rolls, all Zubin wanted to know now was if there was anything from those chicken rolls he could salvage. But he was too polite to ask directly. He opted for a non-confrontational route.

'Umm, okay . . .' he said as he stepped into her apartment. She had unpacked boxes lying around with a blue beanbag plonked in the centre of her living room. A tall lamp on the far-right corner was the only other intruder.

Zubin scanned the sparse room and didn't see any sign of his dinner. As he stood looking, he asked her, 'Listen, so do you have space for these paneer rolls now?' He tried to chuckle along the way.

But Malvika had darted into the bedroom by now. He heard a tap running inside. She was back in the next few seconds with a wooden stool in her hand. 'There you go. That's the only thing I have for you to sit on. Unless you want to sit on the floor. It's squeaky clean. I promise you that.'

'I can see that,' Zubin acknowledged and perched himself on the stool.

'Sorry, you were asking me something when I went in to wash my hands.'

'I was only asking if you have space for these paneer rolls any more,' he chuckled again, holding up the packet.

'What about you? Won't you have them? You aren't lactose intolerant or anything, I hope.'

And only God knows why, but Zubin fibbed. It was perhaps her presence that made him want to hide his imperfections. 'No, not at all. I love paneer. It's just that I had this green coriander chutney downstairs which . . .'

She cut him midway. 'Thank God!' She sighed and continued. 'That makes me feel less guilty. I mean people have such fancy quirks these days,' she said with the tenderness of an old friend. 'When we were growing up, we would have anything our mom served, but try telling that to Saransh, my kid. Oh God! Such a fit he throws!'

'Nice. You have a child. How cool is that!' Zubin betrayed a false sense of excitement. His eyes wandered through the apartment for signs of this kid.

'Yeah, and allergic to paneer apparently. I mean, I have my allergies too, but a kid, all of seven, can you imagine?' she continued.

There were so many things to address in that ramble of hers that Zubin didn't know where to begin. There was an arresting quality to her words and her mannerisms. She moved her thin hands while speaking like she was conducting an extraordinary orchestra for the world to listen to.

While a part of Zubin had forgotten about his own lactose intolerance, another was wrestling with the unpardonable joke that fate was playing on him tonight. How could this dusky diva, his hot new neighbour, come bearing a child.

In his head, he had accepted the dinner of these paneer rolls for himself tonight.

He continued with his polite overture.

'Where is he?' he asked her with a calm air, even as millions of hungry minions cried out from the pit of his stomach.

'In New Delhi, with his grandparents. As a single mother, I have to rely on them all the time. I didn't want to get him here until I was all settled. Gosh, am I telling you too many details? What about you? Where do you work?'

'Ah! There, a sliver of hope,' Zubin thought to himself. 'I am a creative director at Wrights and Stevens. We make ads nobody watches.'

That helped crack a beatific smile on her face. 'You can't be that bad.'

'You have no clue,' he said self-effacingly. 'What about you? Where do you work?'

'Let me set a plate for you first. We can talk through the night. You don't have work tomorrow, do you?'

'No, I don't. But I hope I am not holding you up. You must be tired with the moving in.'

'Who cares! I don't get good neighbours ever. Maybe this is changing. I also have one more chicken roll left in the kitchen, I think. Let me get that for you.'

What a night this was turning out to be. Suddenly.

'Excellent. Let me get that extra packet of green chutney from downstairs then. It just takes that chicken roll to a whole new level.'

Malvika, who was allergic to green chutney herself, thought of stopping Zubin. But his sudden spurt of energy and the guilt that she had eaten half of his dinner held her back.

Hours later, as they talked late into the night about the vagaries of life, there lay on the side a single paper plate that Malvika and Zubin shared.

It now carried the crumpled paper wrap of a paneer roll that Zubin had just devoured. Alongside, there were some hazy remnants of the green chutney that Malvika indulged in.

They were well aware that there would be a price to pay in some form tomorrow but both—for the moment—were willing to suspend their belief, and their allergies, for each other.

Acknowledgements

*B*uffering Love was written over the course of a difficult time in 2016 but having the following people to lean on was everything I needed to wake up each day and put words to paper.

Ben Maraniss, my screenwriting instructor at the New York Film Academy. In every class, a calm Ben Maraniss would walk in with a Starbucks coffee in his hand, flick his frazzled hair and tell us unforgettable stories. In this lifetime, everything I know (or will know) about the craft and science of storytelling can be traced back to Ben.

To Rajat Kapoor, the auteur whose writing sensibility I worship and who took the time to read through my first screenplay. In his sparse office, he capped his sharp two-hour feedback session by telling me, 'You can write. Just keep at it,' and gave me a new lease of life with those words.

Mom and Dad, Viggy's parents for never raising an eyelid when I told them I was trading my plush job at PUMA for a year of uncertainties.

To my Sister, *Ammamma,* for perhaps never comprehending the implications of my decision but quietly praying for me every single day.

To my family back home in Kerala who raised me and even to this day ensure there is quiet in the house, just so that I can scribble on a page or on screen.

To my adopted daughter Merin, that charming twenty-seven-year-old kid I met in PUMA, for reading every word of three different versions of the manuscript through different time zones. Twice. And for sending me copious notes. Countless times.

To Dr Uma Narain, that veritable powerhouse of all things films and literature, who I met at SPJIMR. Knowing her has been an education of a lifetime.

To Joy, for his unwavering attention to every story. He was a lighthouse I could veer to every time I felt this ship needed direction.

To my bunch of friends, philosophers and guides, who read different versions of the book and critiqued it. Sowjanya, Achala, Bhavisha, Mallika, Chiranth and Darius. As a first-time writer, what you seek most is unfiltered feedback, and if it comes in the form of people with a taste as high as theirs, you can consider yourself lucky.

To Dipta and Vikram Sampath, for showing me the way.

To Sneha of Nirvana films, who always had an encouraging word to say and only constructive feedback to offer whenever I approached her.

To those who were always only a call away when I shared a story or a concept and asked for feedback. Shariq, Mahesh, Vidhya, Sammy, Auditya (thanks for that Swamy joke), Barry, Kaus, Sunayna, Nirmal (for the China tip), Sid,

Ronnie, Sowmya. Every time you said something nice or critiqued the book, you made me want to make it better.

To Milee Ashwarya of Penguin Random House, who I approached with a nervous pitch at the Bangalore Literature Festival. The year 2016 was dotted with relentless rejections from publishers, producers and directors alike and she was the last person I pitched the book to in late-December 2016. If she would've said anything other than, 'Sounds interesting, send me an email,' this book wouldn't have happened.

To my most amazing editor, a treasure called Gurveen they have at Penguin Random House. I still have the version of the manuscript with her detailed notes. Her nuanced inputs, her attention to detail and her ability to spot exactly what might make a story better is nonpareil.

To the good folks at Book Bakers and Suhail Mathur, my agent, who to this day sends me detailed voice memos whenever I need a quick input.

To Tushar and the team at HealthifyMe, who gave me a long leash of flexible hours at work for the short while I was there.

To my former bosses, Rashmi, Neeraj, Gowri, Satish, Rajiv, Abhishek. Without the discipline, work ethic and passion I imbibed from you, this would've been a pipe dream.

This might sound strange, but to Pixar, the holy grail of storytelling. To the writers there, none of whom I know or perhaps will meet in this lifetime. But to you guys for inspiring mortals like me through timeless characters like Carl, Ellie, Marlin, Andy, Doc Hudson, Sadness, Riley, Bing Bong, among many others. For setting the bar so high, that it only makes me want to reach for it.

Lastly to Viggy, my effervescent better half. For your unflinching empathy, limitless compassion and undying love. I know I am better for it.

And finally, to love that devastates, enthrals, buffers and outlives us all.